*A
Harlequin
Romance*

OTHER
Harlequin Romances
by JANE DONNELLY

THE MAN IN THE NEXT ROOM

by

JANE DONNELLY

HARLEQUIN BOOKS TORONTO
WINNIPEG

First published in 1970 by Mills & Boon Limited,
17 - 19 Foley Street, London, England.

SBN 373-01462-7

Harlequin Canadian edition published January, 1971
Harlequin U.S. edition published April, 1971

Reprinted 1975

Printed in Canada

CHAPTER ONE

IF I believed in ghosts, thought Sian Rowan, I know what I'd like to ask you. You bewitched a king. Even after three hundred years your advice would be worth having.

But she didn't believe in ghosts, and if Nell Gwynn was haunting anywhere it was unlikely to be the storeroom of a village shop. Once the building had been an inn, local legend said Nell had slept in that room, but her shade could surely find more palatial meanderings than round the packing cases and between the shelves of assorted and entirely mundane merchandise.

All the same it was a nice thought.

When Sian had been brought up here to see the room that might make a bed-sitter the girl showing it had been apologetic. There was a lot still to do, they'd been converting in their spare time, and running the stores didn't leave them much spare time.

But Sian had decided as soon as she met George and Fiona McDade that she would like to live under their roof. She would have taken the room in practically any state.

Langley Hollis had brought her along. He had said, 'This is Miss Rowan, she's going to work in the gallery, but she isn't local so she's needing somewhere to live. You did say you were thinking of letting one of your rooms, didn't you?'

George and Fiona had exchanged glances, George had shrugged, leaving Fiona to say, 'It's a bit stark. We've cleared it and we've painted the walls, and that's about all we have done. You can see it if you like.'

Please, Sian had said, and she had followed Fiona from the ground floor, George's province where he sold everything from humbugs to hacksaws, up through Fiona's floor – toys, wools, children's wear, and a fashion boutique taking in all females from teens to octogenarians.

The building was three-storey Tudor. It had been a small

coaching inn when the road outside was a one-carriage-wide track. Not that the road was much wider now, and the village hadn't grown all that much either.

All the way up the winding staircase to the room under the eaves Fiona was preparing her. 'The top floor are the storerooms. We've cleared one and we did talk of taking in a lodger, but we've hardly started on the place.'

The stairs were uneven, and so were the dark boards of the flooring. Racks of dresses stood on the landing and piles of wellington boots, and Fiona opened a door and said, 'See what I mean.'

The walls were white between the beautiful black beams. The window was high, but light streamed through.

Sian said, 'It's lovely.'

Fiona laughed, 'It's clean, and that's about all you can say for it.'

'I'll take it,' said Sian.

'Good,' said Fiona. 'When do you want to move in?'

'Next week-end? Mr. Hollis said I could start at the gallery right away, I just have to clear up a few things.'

'Right,' said Fiona. 'There's a divan bed, chairs, table. George'll get those up for us as soon as the shop shuts. Then I'll put you a curtain across Nelly's room.'

An open archway connected with the next room, and through it Sian glimpsed packing cases. She asked, 'Who's Nelly?' and when she was told she said, 'Don't bother about a curtain. Well, not till winter comes. I should enjoy having a bed-sitter that was part of a room where Nell Gwynn slept.'

That was three months ago. Nothing had stirred in the small hours in Nelly's room but a mouse, and that turned out to be the field variety, and was carried downstairs by George on Fiona's insistence and set free through the back door.

Still, if Nell Gwynn's shade did return Sian would have been very willing to take lessons from it in man-appeal. Langley Hollis might not have been Nell Gwynn's type. Nell had been a practical-minded girl and Langley was an artist and a dreamer, but Sian was in love with him.

She had been from that first day. The advertisement had said, 'Assistant needed for art and antiques gallery in picturesque Shropshire village. Small but thriving business.'

She had phoned the number on impulse. She was looking for a new job, so she had rung for more details and liked the sound of the man who spoke to her. She had liked the sound of the job too, and come down to see, and looked at him and felt her heart turn over.

Langley Hollis was tall and fairish, clear-cut features, a sensitive mouth, and an immediate impression of kindness and sincerity that made you feel you had known him a long time.

He had explained what the work would entail, dealing with customers, a few clerical duties, and she had thought yes, yes, yes. 'Have you had any previous experience in this kind of business?' he had asked, and she had hedged, 'I went to art school, but – well, no, I haven't. I was a salesgirl, but I sold hats.'

'You went to art school? Wasn't working in a hat shop a waste of your training?'

She had thought so herself at times, but an artist, even the small-time artist she would have been if she'd taken the job the advertising agency offered her when she left art school, has to put work first, and Sian couldn't.

She said, 'My aunt – she'd reared me, I lived with her – became ill. She needed nursing, so I could only take a part-time job. She died last month.'

Langley Hollis looked as though he understood and sympathized, then he asked, 'When could you start? If ever a man needed an assistant I do,' and she could hardly bear to leave.

She had, of course, to give in her notice and collect her belongings, but she begrudged the wasted days until she could get back again.

She had liked her old job well enough, but it had been second-best in every way. She had taken it for no other reason than Aunt Mary, because the shop was near enough to the flat for Sian to slip back every hour or so and reassure herself that all was well.

It hadn't been in any way a snappy hat shop. The styles were all variations on classic themes. The clientele of Madame Hélène had been coming to her for years, and as they were all her own age group they would probably be buying hats as long as she was selling them. There had been no question of planning for the future by luring in the next generation.

Madame Hélène – Mrs. Helen Griggs – was a friend of Aunt Mary's, and she had been a very considerate employer, sharing Sian's grief as Aunt Mary weakened, helping at the end in every way she could.

After the funeral she had said, 'You know that if you want a full-time job, dear, you can come to me full-time.' Sian had to earn a living. They had just managed with Aunt Mary's pension and Sian's small wage. Now of course Sian needed a full-time job, but not in the little hat shop. She had thanked Mrs. Griggs and said she would be giving up the flat, and possibly moving away. 'I feel I need a change of scene. A new town, a new job. You've been very kind, but you do understand, don't you?'

Mrs. Griggs did. Mary had reared Sian from a baby, all the same it wasn't every girl who would have repaid her with such love and so much care. Helen Griggs said so. She wished Sian well, she would be sorry to lose her, but it was high time Sian had some sort of life of her own, time she met a nice boy, because she would make a wonderful wife.

Sian had smiled at that, and said she was thinking more of being a career girl for a while. 'And why not?' Mrs. Griggs had said. 'But I still think your vocation is looking after somebody else. I still think the man who gets you is going to be so lucky.'

Sian had dreamed her dreams, of course. She had had no social life at all for the two years of Aunt Mary's illness, but she had dreamed, and Langley Hollis was so near the man who had walked through her dreams that it was uncanny.

She had known before the end of her first day of working

8

for him that Mrs. Griggs was right. Her vocation was looking after someone else, and she wanted it to be Langley.

She never bothered with breakfast. There was a gas-ring in her room, and she had unhampered access to Fiona's kitchen. But she always had coffee over at the Little Gallery, with Langley, and the day didn't really start until then.

She paused in the doorway of her bed-sitter to look back. There was no reason why she had to leave the room bandbox-neat, bedclothes hidden in the scarlet-painted cabin trunk she used as an occasional table, make-up tidy on the shelf under the mirror, even the rugs set straight. She would be coming back to this room alone, and if she didn't no one was likely to be marking it for neatness.

But disorder bothered her. Unobtrusive and neat-fingered, she tidied as she went, and now she gave the room a final swift inspection before she closed the door after her. She was a tall girl, with long long legs, brown eyes, and red-brown hair worn loose and shoulder-length. She wore a pink shirt-waister dress, sandals on her bare feet, and she ran downstairs, calling ''Morning' as she passed the open kitchen door where Fiona was cutting toast and George was poking the overnight ashes out of the boiler.

Their 'hellos' sounded as though they were both yawning. It was nearly a quarter to nine, and that was the time the shop opened. The first and only queue of the day was already forming on the pavement outside, the children who would get on to the school bus at ten minutes to nine, and poured in as soon as George opened the door and headed for the nothing-over-sixpence sweet counter.

'He's coming,' Sian assured them.

The Little Gallery was at the other end of the village street, but that only made it a couple of minutes' walk away. The gallery was nowhere near as old as the village stores. It had been built around the turn of the century, a flat-fronted building, a central door opening directly on to the pavement, and huge windows that gave an excellent view of the contents of the showroom.

The showroom was the width of the building. Pictures

hung on the walls: all sorts, from modern to Victorian oils. There was furniture, most of it missed being antiques, but it was all attractive and fairly priced; and a great deal of bric-à-brac. It was a pleasant place, to browse through or work in, and Sian turned her key in the door with a glow she felt every morning. She liked stepping into the shop, the smell of paint and polish; and knowing that Langley was behind that door at the far end always quickened her step, so that she deliberately checked herself, otherwise she would have ended running.

She picked up the post that lay on the mat, and glanced at it. Three typewritten envelopes, two handwritten. All for Langley. One of the handwritten was in a black bold hand, and that was on top when she laid them on the kitchen table.

Langley was not down yet – they opened at nine, but Sian was here, and Emily had his breakfast ready and coffee on the table.

Emily was a round and motherly soul. She had been twenty-five years younger when she first came to work here, but she hadn't looked so very different from the way she looked today. She smiled, seeing Sian, and rolled her eyes upwards. 'Overslept again,' she said. Two women in a man's world, content with the natural order of things. 'I don't know,' said Emily. 'Coffee?'

'Please.' There was a cup set for Sian, and she filled it, and sat down and sipped. She said, 'I can open the shop. There isn't likely to be a mad rush of customers.' Emily chuckled tolerantly, 'It'd be all the same if there was, wouldn't it?' She looked down at the letters, and picked up the one with the black handwriting. 'Barney,' she said.

She held it at arm's length as if it was a photograph. 'He can't be feeling too bad. He's written that plain enough.' She went out into the hall and called, 'Letter from Barney here' up the stairs, then came back and waited, holding the letter in impatient fingers as though she could twitch the news out of it.

Sian said, 'He was lucky, wasn't he?'

'Born lucky,' said Emily. 'If they dropped him off a cliff he'd land soft.'

Barney was Langley's younger brother and just over a month ago he had been involved in a car pile-up when a tyre burst on a motorway. He should have been killed – looking at the car everybody was agreed on that – but he wasn't, and neither was anybody else.

Right from the beginning Emily had insisted that Barney would be all right. A phone call had notified Langley and he had turned grey-faced to Sian and Emily. 'Barney's had a car crash. He – he's dying.'

Sian had never met Barney. She had heard about him, he was a T.V. writer, he lived in London, and she whispered, 'No, oh no.'

'I don't believe it,' Emily had said.

That was reflex reaction to tragic news, but Emily meant it literally. Langley had gone to the hospital, George McDade had taken him; it was the best part of a hundred miles away, and in that state of mind he would have been a road hazard himself.

While he was away the village hummed with the news. Barney Hollis had been born and reared here, as Langley had. Everyone had heard and everyone was worried. They phoned and they came round, and Emily kept saying, 'He'll pull through – you see.'

She was right. Langley rang from the hospital to tell them that Barney had multiple injuries, had needed and had had surgery. It was natural that Langley should be more shocked and less sanguine than George, who took over the phone from him and said, 'He's going to make it. He's going to be all right.'

'I knew it,' Emily had said. 'That one's got more lives than a cat.'

Now this was Barney's first letter. The progress reports had continued well; Barney Hollis obviously healed at a good brisk rate, and although Langley was still worried about him and made regular phone calls for reassurance, here was a letter, and as Emily had said, he'd written that name and address with a steady hand,

Langley came hurrying in. 'Here we are,' said Emily. 'What's he got to say for himself?'

Langley ripped open the envelope and took out the single sheet and read rapidly, 'Coming out of hospital ... everything under control ...' his eyes skimmed ahead. 'He's coming down here for a bit.'

'That's nice,' said Emily. 'Got to take it easy, I suppose.'

Langley smiled, 'I wonder how long that'll last. Well, you'd better get his room ready.'

'The room's there,' said Emily. 'It's always ready.'

The house that incorporated the Little Gallery was a good-sized one. There were four bedrooms, and one of them was Barney's room. When he'd lived here it must have contained personal belongings, but it was six years since Barney Hollis had left the village and Sian gathered that his visits had been few and far between. There was no longer anything in that room but the items you would find in a hotel bedroom.

She had helped to dust the room, on one of Emily's lumbago days, and she had asked, 'Do they see much of each other?'

That was just before the accident, and Emily had said regretfully, 'No. Different sort of lives they lead. Langley was always the responsible one. Family ties didn't mean so much to Barney.'

They did when he was in trouble. Now he needed help he was willing enough to come back to the quiet little village and let Emily and Langley look after him.

Sian was curious to see him, and more than slightly prejudiced against him. For one thing she knew that the Little Gallery had been left by their father to his sons jointly, and although Barney never did a hand's turn for the business he still took his cut of the profits. That might be legal, but it didn't seem fair.

She drank her coffee, while Langley ate his breakfast and opened the rest of the mail, and thought that she wouldn't mind the chance to tell Barney Hollis she didn't think it was fair. It wasn't as though he needed the money, he was a successful script-writer. His name was always turning up on the small screen.

His name was also on the business letterheads, under Langley's as partner. That was how Sian first heard of him, on her first day. Langley had smiled a little ruefully. 'My brother,' he'd explained. 'The sleeping partner.'

Fiona had told her that the gallery had been left jointly to the brothers, and Sian had asked, 'Does Barney do anything in the business?'

'Shouldn't think so,' Fiona had said. 'He couldn't get out of it fast enough, as I recall.' She and George had laughed together. 'There used to be such rows,' said Fiona. 'Old Mr. Hollis used to tell everybody that Barney would be the death of him. He used to say, "There are times when I cannot believe that boy is my son. Still less can I believe he was the son of my dear wife".'

Fiona was smiling, but Sian said, 'That sounds dreadful.'

'It does,' Fiona agreed cheerfully, 'but it wasn't. I'm sure he never meant it. But Barney was the wild one; half the time nobody knew what he was going to get up to next. He didn't give a hoot.'

Now Langley put aside the business letters he had opened and picked up the letter from Barney again. He said to Sian, 'I'm still worried about him.'

She felt that was probably the habit of a lifetime. She could imagine Langley, the sensitive responsible elder brother sharing his father's concern while Barney ran wild, and what must have been his father's heartache when Barney left home and showed how little family ties had ever meant to him.

She said, 'Why should you worry about him? He's getting well again and he's coming back here to be looked after. He's got it made.'

'That's what worries me,' said Langley, 'that he should be coming back here. He has plenty of friends, men and women. I'm sure he could have gone to most of them to convalesce and he could more than pay his way. In the last six years he's never stayed in this village for longer than three consecutive days, not even when our father died. He must be feeling pretty low to choose us and this backwater.'

'He probably is,' said Sian. 'And from what I've heard that might do him no harm.'

Langley looked at her keenly and she coloured. This was a small village. In the little time Sian had been there she had heard enough gossip to fill a very libellous book, and since Barney Hollis's accident she had been regaled with a host of reminiscences on that young man.

The picture was engaging enough, unless you were his family. With his family he had been, she felt, brutally selfish. It might have been having no mother. Mrs. Hollis had died when Barney was born, and Emily and friends and neighbours had helped in the upbringing of the two small boys. But from all accounts Mr. Hollis was a good father, and Langley had grown into a kind and generous man. It was Barney who had taken everything and given nothing.

She hoped she was wrong, but she suspected that if Langley had been injured Barney might have been shocked and sorry, but he wouldn't be showing half this concern.

Langley had never said a word against Barney. Come to that most of the gossip had been wryly admiring, but Sian had made her own assessment and in her book it added up to a very self-centred man.

She said defensively, 'I don't care what you say, he's lucky to have you and Emily willing to take him in and look after him.'

'It's half his house,' said Langley. He smiled at her. 'And he is my brother.'

'I know,' said Sian. She got up. 'I'll open up, shall I?' she said.

'I'll be right with you,' said Langley. His eyes fell again to the letter.

Sian turned the key and the Little Gallery was open for

custom. There were no customers waiting to get in, this early there rarely were, but cars would stop during the day as someone passed and found the glimpse they'd got in transit intriguing. Regular customers would return, and some would come on recommendations, because the Little Gallery had its small reputation.

Sian dusted some glassware, rearranged the paperweights on top of the Victorian boudoir writing table – just for the fun of it, the first arrangement had been fine. Then she went into the studio.

Two doors led from the end of the showroom, one into the house, the other into a huge room called the studio, and serving as a workroom too. Pictures were painted in here, but mostly it was used for reconditioning the furniture that came this way, stripping off veneers of dirt and varnish, strengthening, repairing, re-upholstering.

Langley did all that, and he did it well with care and skill. Sian loved to watch how he brought beauty back to neglected things. He was teaching her and she was learning quickly. He said she was. He said she had natural talent, and he said often that he didn't know how he had managed before she came.

That was something. She was appreciated, and it was early days yet. She was satisfied to know that she was the most important girl in his life, even if it was only a very platonic relationship.

He was so good-looking that women customers often perked up visibly when he walked towards them. Sian had watched matronly tourists with gimlet eyes for a bargain turn into southern belles under Langley Hollis's smile.

That was good for business. If he had been less scrupulous it might have been even better, because whatever they bought from the Little Gallery was worth the money they paid for it. Langley Hollis might never be a rich man, but he would always be an honest man.

And Sian loved him. She had never been in love before. At art school she had had a crush on another student who didn't know she existed even when he was talking to her.

She had overheard her name mentioned when there was an epidemic of 'flu about. Someone had said, 'Sian Rowan went down with it a couple of weeks back,' and he had asked, 'Who's she?'

The boy who had said her name had floundered trying to describe her, as though no feature or characteristic came strongly enough to mind. 'Tallish,' he'd said.

She was older now. She knew that she no longer melted into the background, that her figure was adequate, and her face was attractive if not memorable, and it was no impossible dream that one day Langley Hollis might fall in love with her.

Emily thought he would. She hadn't said so in so many words, but she had talked about other girls. Not many girls, they came down to two. One had married somebody else – it hadn't broken Langley's heart, said Emily. He'd felt it for a bit, but it was four or five years ago, and you should see her now, he was well out of that. The other was young Phyllis Barker, from Woodgrange Farm, and she was a silly little thing. Emily had clucked her tongue at Phyllis's silliness. She wasn't right for him at all, and he knew it. She used to phone up and hang around, but – Emily grimaced – she'd got herself another lad now, and good luck to him.

Emily looked approvingly at Sian, and as Sian helped around the house and took to the work of running the gallery with flair and fervour Emily grew more approving daily.

A battery-powered bell, connected with the front door, rang in the studio when anyone came into the shop, so it was all right to close the studio door and get on with your work in there. Sian slipped on a paint-smeared smock and rolled up her sleeves. She was enjoying her current task. Langley had bought a rocking horse that had spent the last fifty years in an attic. Before it had been hot favourite with what must have been a large and energetic family of children because its paintwork had been worn through, its mane had been pulled out, and it had carried the scars of battle. Langley had restored it to its original basic shape and now Sian was putting back the colours. It was going to be a splendid horse again, and she was becoming increasingly fond of it.

Once its spots had been scarlet on white; the white was done, hard and gleaming, and today she was starting on the spots. She was opening the tin of paint when Langley came in and she looked up and smiled. 'I'll be sorry when we lose him. Isn't he a beauty?'

'He certainly is,' Langley walked around him. 'If we stick him in the window he'll be an eye-catcher.'

Sian stroked the long silky mane. 'And he'll sell so fast, and that's a pity.'

Langley was carrying the morning mail. They always went over it together at this stage, and Sian typed out the letters that needed answering. Aunt Mary had insisted on that secretarial course running alongside Sian's art school studies, and now both skills were being used, Sian was realizing her potential. It was a marvellous feeling.

They dealt with the letters, one of them was asking Langley to make an offer for some dining chairs. 'I'll ring them,' he said, 'and I might as well go over right away.' It was a nearby town and a family he had dealt with before.

A couple had lived all their married life in the house and among the furniture left to them by his parents. Not junk by any means but not heirloom quality either, and now their children had reached the hypercritical age and bit by bit the old stuff was being replaced by modern designs.

As far as Langley could remember those dining chairs were walnut and rather pretty, and he had no doubt he could find customers for them.

Another letter contained a photograph of a small child with a smug and secret smile. It was addressed to Langley, but this was Sian's department and she looked at it critically. 'When do they want it?' she asked.

'As soon as possible. It's for the grandmother's birthday on the twenty-second, so it's a rush job. Can you manage it?'

'Of course.' She looked regretfully at her tin of paint and the rocking horse. 'I'll get down to it right away.'

The housewife who owned the dining chairs would be in

all morning and the sooner the better she said, now they'd decided. If Mr. Hollis would like to call that would be quite convenient.

Sian was often left in charge of the gallery. Langley had to get his stock before he could sell it; that meant attending every auction that showed promise, going anywhere if there was a chance of picking up something for the gallery. She had learned the prices of everything in her first few days; there had been one assistant, Emily told her, who'd disposed of a Georgian candlestick from a pair for twenty-five shillings. Sian coped easily enough; this was of necessity a leisurely trade. No one came in who didn't have time to look and consider. She had never been rushed off her feet at Madame Hélène's, and here the tempo was even slower.

She took the photograph that had arrived in the morning mail over to the corner of the studio where she did her painting. For the first time since she left art school she was painting for profit. She had amused herself at home painting and sketching, but she hadn't much confidence in it, it had just been a hobby.

Langley painted. There was a half-finished picture of his on an easel now and he had real talent. Landscapes mostly, lovely wide vistas of the countryside around that sold well. His father had been an artist too. Some of Jonathan Hollis's paintings hung in the drawing-room of the house and you could trace the family likeness in the treatment. Langley and his father must have had a great deal in common, Sian felt. She wished she could have known Mr. Hollis, he sounded a wonderful man.

In a studio again of course she had wanted to paint, and she had tried a watercolour and shown it to Langley, and he had said, 'That's very good.'

She'd smiled, 'I knew pretty soon that I was never likely to be any great shakes as an artist, but it's nice to be dabbling in paint.' She had copied one of the miniatures in the display room, and she'd copied with meticulous care, and that was how this started, painting miniatures from photographs. The one in this morning's post would be her third.

Someone had seen one of the previous two and decided that a picture of Melinda Ann would be lovely for grandmother, and it was to be framed in one of the little oval frames of enamelled forget-me-nots.

Sian began to copy Melinda Ann's round and dimpled face. A pretty child, and the smile gave character to the photograph. 'I'll bet you're doted on,' thought Sian. Five years of cherishing could well be the background of so much smugness in one so young.

She worked on through the morning. Emily brought her in some coffee and biscuits around eleven, and there were several callers. Not all of them customers, but even the ones who looked and went away were welcome because they might come again and buy next time.

Around lunch time Sian set Melinda Ann aside and decided to give the rocking horse a few spots. It would make a change and the miniature was coming on so well that she felt justified in amusing herself for half an hour. They weren't giving him quite such pillar-box red spots as his original painter. More of a bright pink, but it was a gorgeous colour and Sian dipped her brush in the tin with sensuous glee.

It looked good. She painted with concentration because these spots needed a sharp outline, and she had completed half a dozen in assorted sizes when someone immediately behind her said, 'What are you doing to that poor horse?' right in her ear so that she jumped and the brush flicked and one spot ended with a tail like a flying comet.

The man had a beaten-up look: an arm in a sling, a hardly-healed scar down the side of his face, and a number of fading bruises where they showed and probably where they didn't. But his eyes didn't look beaten up, they were gleaming with amusement, and Sian said, 'The battery on the door bell must have run down.'

It had rung for some customers ten minutes ago, but she hadn't heard him come in. He nodded, 'That figures.'

Of course she knew who he was. She said, without enthusiasm, 'You'll be Barney.'

'Right, and you will be the redoubtable Miss Rowan.'

He made her sound like a battleship. She said stiffly, 'I am Miss Rowan.'

'I hear you're running the business these days.'

She was not, and she wondered who had said that she was. Then she realized that Langley had probably mentioned her, talking to Barney on the phone, and said she was a help. But he certainly wouldn't have said she was running the business. She said sharply, 'Don't be ridiculous.'

He grinned, 'Look who's talking! Do you always wear a pink moustache?'

She got up to look in the mirror. She must have wiped her hand across her face because she had a bright pink smudge just under her nose. She looked like a clown. Cool dignity wasn't going to cut much ice while she looked like this. She felt her lips twitch on a giggle; and behind her the man laughed too. She disapproved of him, but he had an infectious laugh, it was hard not to join in, and she did look ridiculous with her pink moustache.

She said, 'What if it won't come off?' and grabbed a turpentined rag and began to dab away, still laughing.

Langley came in at that stage. He stood in the doorway for a moment, unsmiling, his eyes on them both. Then he said, 'I almost fell over your case. How did you come?'

'Taxi,' said Barney.

'You didn't say it would be today.'

'Does it matter?'

'No, no, of course not. You're welcome any time, you know that. I see you've introduced yourself to Sian.'

'We recognized each other on sight,' said Barney, and Langley said, 'Good,' and, with incredulous delight, Sian thought – he's jealous. Langley is jealous that we were laughing together, so that has to mean I mean something to him.

CHAPTER TWO

LANGLEY smiled suddenly. 'And how are you feeling, you old reprobate?'

'Pretty good,' said Barney.

'You were lucky.'

'That's a fact,' said Barney.

'Does Emily know you've arrived?'

'No, I came in here, I thought you might be around.' He grinned at Sian. 'I'd better report to Emily. See both of you later?'

'You'll see a lot of us later,' said Langley.

There was affection between the brothers. Sian sensed it, a warm, comfortable feeling. They seemed so unalike, Langley with his sensitive artist's face, and Barney who looked neither artistic nor particularly sensitive. Although there was a line to the mouth as though most of the time he was amused, or impatient, or something that might be intriguing.

So unalike, but fond of each other. As Barney went out Sian asked Langley, 'Any joy with the chairs?'

'I brought them back. They're in good condition, I think we'll do well on them.'

'Lovely,' she said. 'May I see?'

The chairs were outside in the estate van and Langley carried them through to the studio. They were nice chairs; the original plush of the seats had worn smooth and dingy, but that was a minor matter.

Sian admired the chairs, and Langley went across to look at the miniature and said it was coming on very well. 'You'll have it finished in time for Grandmother's birthday?'

'I should certainly hope so. Unless something very catastrophic happens.' She smiled, saying that, and still looking at the miniature Langley asked, 'And what did you think of Barney?'

'Much as I'd expected, I suppose. Much as everybody described him.'

'I hope he's going to be all right.'

'What do you mean?' He had had a nasty list of injuries, but you only had to look at him to see he was well on the mend, so why did Langley sound so grave?

Langley said, 'I still don't think he'd have come back here unless he was at a very low ebb.'

She said bluntly, 'Maybe he feels it's about time he did a bit more to earn his cut of the profits.'

She hadn't mentioned that before, it was really none of her business, and as Langley frowned she said, 'Sorry, but everyone knows, don't they? I must have been told a dozen times.'

'I would prefer it if you didn't discuss these things.'

She pushed back her hair from her face before she remembered the paint on her fingers, and went back to the mirror and picked up the turpentined rag again. She didn't have a moustache this time, just one cheek with the flush of high fever. She said, 'I honestly don't discuss your affairs, but this is such a little village and everybody seems to know all about everybody else. And short of snapping their heads off every time they open their mouths what can I do?'

If anyone had said anything derogatory about Langley she would have snapped soon enough, but they didn't. Everybody liked Langley, and they all seemed to like Barney too. The gossip had always been kindly, although more than one had said that Barney was the taker, and Langley the giver.

Langley smiled ruefully, 'I know. I should know, I was born in the place.'

'Anyhow,' she said, 'I promise you that when I gossip back it's only about myself and my small doings. Not about you or the business or anything like that.'

'I'm sure of it,' he said. 'I should imagine you're probably the most loyal person I know.'

She was loyal, to the few friends she had kept during the years of caring for Aunt Mary. Certainly she would be loyal to the man she loved, and she loved Langley although he didn't know it.

She said quietly, 'Thank you.' Then she picked up the tiny brush with which she was painting the miniature and went on with her faithful copy of Melinda Ann's snub nose.

There were no more customers in the next half hour, and no disturbances until Emily looked in to tell them that lunch was served and getting cold.

The gallery closed from one to two and it was past one, but Langley had been engrossed in his dining chairs, and Sian was concentrating on her miniature, and neither of them had glanced at watch or clock for the last ten minutes.

They jumped guiltily – Emily didn't like lunch kept waiting – explaining how they had been carried away so that the time flew by. 'All right,' Emily pardoned them, 'but come on now, then.' She looked at Sian's portrait. 'That's going to be pretty,' she said.

'She's a pretty child,' said Sian.

She went through the showroom to the door leading to the street, to slip on the latch and to turn the OPEN notice to CLOSED, then she hurried after Emily and Langley.

They had the midday meal in the kitchen. The kitchen was roomy and comfortable: a Welsh dresser stocked with willow pattern, sheepskin rugs on polished cherry-red flagstones. The table was long, the chairs old-fashioned wooden wheelbacks. During the winter months there would be a fire burning, but it was summer now and the room was warm from the heat of the cooking stove.

The meal was a steak and kidney pie, and Barney was already half-way through his helping. He smiled on them as they came in, Sian a pace or two behind. He said, 'Emily's pastry is still the best in the world.'

'You should try Sian's,' said Emily. 'She has a beautiful light hand. You should try her Victoria sponge.'

Sian was a good plain cook, and it was nice of Emily to say so, but she doubted if Barney Hollis would rate home cooking very high in his list of irresistible female accomplishments. His kind of girl probably wouldn't know one end of a potato-peeler from the other, but Langley's kind of girl would, and it was Langley's kind of girl Sian wanted to be.

During the meal Emily began to talk about a television play Barney had written for a current and tough series. Emily hadn't liked the sentiments and said so, and Barney grinned at her when she complained, 'It wasn't a bit true to life. Folk just don't carry on that way.'

'Oh, but they do,' said Barney.

Sian felt he was laughing at all three of them. Emily probably didn't mind, and neither did Sian, but it wasn't fair that Barney should come the blasé cosmopolitan with Langley, who had every bit as much talent as he had and very likely more.

She said, 'Have you seen Langley's painting? The one he's doing now of Deniston Crag.'

It had been in the studio when Barney came in this morning, but she didn't think he had noticed it, and now he asked Langley, 'Have I?'

'I think so,' said Langley. 'I was just starting it last time you were down.'

It wasn't a picture that could be hurried, and of course Langley had so many other things to do – like six more chairs to be re-upholstered from this morning – but by talking about his painting Sian hoped she was reminding Barney that his brother was an artist, not just a village shopkeeper. And the Little Gallery was no ordinary shop. She talked about some of the things they had right now, beautiful things from a time when the pace of living was slower and more gracious, and Barney listened, and she didn't care if he was humouring her, why should they all talk about his work, why not about Langley's?

She said, 'That rocking horse I was painting this morning, you should have seen that when it came in, and now isn't it gorgeous?'

'It looked splendid,' Barney agreed, and Emily said she

24

remembered having one like it when she was a child, and Langley explained that they had considered putting it in the window to catch the eye of the passers-by.

Barney said, 'If the passer-by is at the wheel of a car, and sees a great horse with pink spots, you don't think there's any danger of him coming through the window?'

He might still be laughing at them, or it could be with them. Sian hoped for the kinder, she said, 'Maybe we could put up one of those warning notices along the road. Instead of "Beware, Cattle Crossing" ours could read, "Pink-spotted Horse Rampant".'

'Is he rampant?' asked Barney.

'Ever so rampant!' said Sian. Barney laughed and she laughed with him, and realized suddenly that Langley was not laughing. Like this morning he was looking at them, quite grave. Barney followed her glance, then he pushed aside his plate, empty now, and got up. 'I think I'll take a walk round the village,' he said.

'Are you up to it?' Langley asked.

'It's not going to be a cross-country trek, more of a short stagger.'

'Had all you want?' said Emily. 'Not even a cup of tea?'

'Somebody's bound to offer me a cup of tea, in my condition.'

Langley said, 'I suppose so. When do we see you back?'

Barney shrugged, 'Don't bother about me, I'll be back some time. And don't bother about meals, Emily love, I'm still nuts on baked beans.'

Emily shook her head disapprovingly, but she said nothing, and when the door closed behind Barney and Langley protested, 'He's supposed to be convalescing, and that means rest and the right food,' she said, 'Stop worrying about him. Those days are over, and you could worry yourself into the ground for all the good it would do.'

Good advice, thought Sian, excellent advice. She asked, 'Shall I make the tea?' because she usually did make it at lunch time.

If Barney returned during the afternoon he didn't look into the studio. The shop bell wasn't ringing, George and Fiona stocked batteries and Sian said she'd bring one with her in the morning. In the meantime they left the studio door open and Sian worked on her miniature where she could see through into the showroom. She didn't see Barney, although he might have passed by while she had her eyes on her work. Customers could be relied on to cough and shuffle if they could see an assistant and were getting no assistance.

A young couple bought a fat white cupid perched on the edge of a candy dish, and looking as though he ate altogether too many candies. And there was a flurry of Americans, five in all but seeming to fill the shop as they roamed and ranged, picking up and putting down. They went out with an average of two small purchases each, and altogether it was a good afternoon.

There had been a call for Barney right after lunch. Langley took it and a girl said she was glad to hear he'd arrived and her name was Natalie, and tell Barney, would he? She had a clear carrying voice so that Sian could hear almost every word, and when Langley put down the phone she said, 'Do you think we should try to find him? He might have wanted to talk to her.'

Langley smiled. 'I'll tell Emily to tell him, and she'll ring again, they always do.'

'Like that, is it?' said Sian lightly.

'Yes,' said Langley, and he looked directly at her as though he hoped she was taking mental note of this. She thought – you don't need to warn me that girls make fools of themselves over your brother. But it was nice to think he was protecting her.

The Little Gallery closed at half five, the village stores at six, so that when Sian went home Fiona and George were still at work. On the ground floor George was serving, and on the next floor Fiona was all but buried in knitting wool, trying to match a green jumper on which someone had miscalculated. Both were busy, and neither noticed Sian.

She went up the stairs to the top floor and her bed-sitter. She enjoyed coming home, everything where she had left it, clean and orderly and bright. She kicked off her sandals, and stretched languorously, her arms above her head. She'd have a bath before she thought about tea. There was a good half hour before either Fiona or George would want the bathroom, and it had been a warm and grubby day.

She untied her belt and began to unbutton her shirtwaister dress. She was on the third button down when Barney Hollis said, 'I suppose I should warn you you're not alone.'

He stood in the doorway of Nelly's room, and she clutched her dress at the throat and croaked, 'You again! That's the second time today you've given me heart failure.'

He nodded as though she had made a point, 'It does seem to be becoming a habit.'

'A habit you'd do well to kick in both our interests.' She rebuttoned her dress. 'Because if it goes on I shall either drop dead from fright or hit out. What are you doing in there anyway?'

He said, 'Working.'

'Doing what? I shouldn't have thought you were up to moving packing cases.'

'Writing.'

'In George's storeroom?'

He corrected her, 'In Nelly's room.'

'That was three hundred years ago, and only for one night, and it probably isn't true.'

'Of course it's true.' He eyed her sadly. 'How cynical can you get? You've been living here for three months, sleeping a few yards away, and you tell me you don't believe Nell Gwynn was here.' He stepped back, waving a hand at the room behind him. 'The place quivers with atmosphere.'

She walked to the archway, seeing boxes and racks of goods that would be needed soon, and things put by to wait for their season: winter wear, toys and crackers and Christmas decorations.

There was no hint left of the room it had once been,

unless you furnished it from your imagination with the four-poster bed, dark oak cupboards and chest, rugs on the floor and candles flaring. Then you could see Nell, white shoulders and the glory of tumbled red hair. Sian said, 'It probably isn't true, but I've always hoped it is.'

'That's a start.' He sounded approving. 'Carry on like that and you'll believe it in no time at all.'

The window in this room had a step up to it so that you could look out. You couldn't from Sian's room where the window was roughly on the same level. Now she saw a table and a chair on the window platform, a typewriter on the table, a tape-recorder on the floor, and she said wonderingly, 'You really are working in here.'

'That's what I told you. You don't believe anything, do you?'

'But why, when it's so inconvenient? Why don't you work at home?'

'Because I prefer to work here.'

That was no explanation and she persisted, '*Why?*'

He said, 'When I first started writing George's father let me use this room. I used to come over here and scribble away and nobody bothered me. Nobody but George and his parents knew where I was.' He leered. 'Nell Gwynn,' he said, 'was my first inspiration.'

'I believe that,' said Sian. She remembered, 'A girl called Natalie phoned. Is she your inspiration now?'

'At times, but in my fashion I'm still true to Nell.'

All very well, but Sian wasn't sure she wanted him writing his play in what was more or less an extension of her bed-sitter. He said obligingly, 'We could build a wall with packing cases.'

'Mmm,' she said. 'What sort of hours do you keep in your business?'

'Reasonable ones, for a while at any rate.'

If he had been any concern of hers she thought she would have tried to stop him working again so soon. She did say, 'Aren't you supposed to be convalescing? Doesn't that mean resting?'

'Not necessarily. The doctors gave me a choice for the next month or so; I can stop working or stop racketing round. I need the money, so I need to work, and this seemed a good place to cut out the distractions.'

She said, 'A nice little backwater! That's what Langley said. He was worried when you decided to come here, he thought you must be at a pretty low ebb. Are you at a pretty low ebb?'

Of course he wasn't. Except physically, and that was a very temporary state of affairs. He was just using his family and friends, and nobody need worry about Barney Hollis. He said indignantly, 'Of course I am. When I have to stop racketing around I'm at a pretty low ebb.'

'Mmm,' she said again, and she heard Fiona's light footsteps racing up the uncarpeted stairs. Fiona shot through the bed-sitter door and stopped, seeing Sian and Barney in the archway to Nelly's room.

'I thought you'd got past,' said Fiona. 'I wanted to catch you before you came up.'

Sian said, 'It might have been as well if you had. I was starting to strip off for a bath.'

Fiona clapped a hand to her mouth. 'Oh no! How far did you get?'

'Only three buttons,' said Sian, and Fiona began to laugh.

'As the old song goes – heaven will protect the working girl.'

'Heaven had nothing to do with it,' said Barney with dignity. 'I spoke up like a gentleman.'

'No!' Fiona fell back a step in theatrical surprise. 'George isn't going to believe this. You're going to appear in an entirely new light in George's eyes, Barney.'

Barney sighed, 'No excitement, the doctor said. A quiet life. Remind George I'm an invalid, will you? You can also tell him that Sian's threatened if I pop up again without warning she's liable to lash out. In my state of health a good backhander could finish me.'

Sian said, 'Don't think you're lulling me into a false sense of security. No backhander would finish you. Emily said if someone pushed you off a cliff you'd make a soft landing.'

Fiona nodded agreement, and Barney said, 'That's nice! That's real sympathy for a man who's on a prescription of all work and no play for the next six months.'

'*Six* months?' Sian queried.

He shrugged. 'Six ... three ... what's a month or two between friends?'

'When the friend's sharing my bed-sitter,' said Sian, 'it can be a talking point.'

Of course he wasn't sharing her bed-sitter, and this was only nonsense they were talking. She didn't flatter herself she would ever be in any danger where Barney Hollis was concerned. He said pleadingly, 'You can't turn me out of Nelly's room. I'll keep office hours. I tell you what – you know those little weather houses, Fair and Foul, where the man comes out and the woman goes in. That's how we'll operate. As soon as you step in through your door I'll walk out of mine.'

She could see that happening if he was really into his work. She could just see herself leaning over the typewriter in mid-sentence and saying, 'Out now, I've come home.' And this wasn't the room they rented they were discussing. It was George and Fiona's storeroom and they could fill it with whatever they liked, and Sian had no say in the matter.

It was considerate of Fiona to ask quite seriously, 'Do you mind, Sian?'

'Of course not,' said Sian, and both Fiona and Barney looked as relieved as though her word was final.

'Thank you,' said Barney.

'Good,' said Fiona, 'and I will get that curtain up to-night.'

'Give me the stuff,' said Sian, 'and I'll sew it.' She was certainly going to need a curtain. She said, 'I hope Nelly continues to provide inspiration.'

'She will,' said Barney. 'She's a girl after my own heart.'

Sian went downstairs with Fiona. She would have her

bath later; right now she thought she'd get a cup of tea. There was tinned food up in her room, and she had a shelf of Fiona's fridge. The McDades' living accommodation was on the same floor as Fiona's section of the store, and Fiona stood in the kitchen doorway in case any late customers came up from the ground floor.

None did while Sian boiled her kettle, and cut and buttered a malt loaf. They talked of Barney Hollis. Fiona had known he used to work in the storeroom. 'But I didn't know he'd want to work there again. Anyhow George said yes, and he won't bother you, will he? I mean you're out all day, and it'll only be during the daytime he'll be working. If you like George could put a real door up in the archway.'

Sian buttered the bread thick. She said, 'You don't really think there's any risk of Barney breaking in on me, do you?'

'Heavens, *no*!' said Fiona. She said it with such certainty that Sian hid a smile. The emphasis wasn't flattering, although it was meant as reassurance. Fiona didn't see Sian as any sort of distraction in Barney Hollis's working schedule.

She remembered Natalie, whose voice had sounded clear and confident, a girl used to making herself heard. He hadn't even bothered to phone her back. Sian said, 'I reckon Nell Gwynn might have been the girl for him.'

Fiona giggled, 'Wouldn't it have been high treason or something, making a pass at Nell Gwynn?'

'With his luck,' said Sian, 'he'd have got away with it.'

George came up the stairs from the ground floor. 'Tea ready?' he said.

'At one minute past six?' said Fiona. 'Put the kettle on again and it soon will be. And Sian did go up to her room without being told Barney was there, and guess what happened?'

'What?' said George.

'Nothing,' said Sian.

'There's a let-down,' said George. 'Have you cut that bread and butter for me?'

'No,' said Sian, and she picked up the tray. 'But you can take a slice to be going on with.'

George took two. 'She doesn't feed me, you know,' he said.

'May you be forgiven,' said Fiona, fishing sausages, chops, ham and eggs out of the fridge and preparing to cook the evening meal.

Sian set the tray down on her 'table' and went quietly to the archway. She looked into the storeroom without speaking. Barney sat at the window, but he wasn't typing, or dictating into that little black microphone. He was chin in hand, and if he was thinking about his work she didn't aim to disturb. If he had frowned or stared blankly she wouldn't have said a word, she'd have moved back and got on with her tea. But he said 'Hi!' amiably enough, so she asked, 'Do you want a cup?'

'Thanks.' He got up and came towards her. 'Am I being invited in?'

'Formally,' she said, and he stepped through the archway from the bare boards to the ones that had been sanded smooth and oiled to a light oak. Her carpeting was a large haircord square, on which stood the scarlet cabin trunk she used as a table. Her bed was a divan with black and white cushions and red tubular arms, and there were a couple of wickerwork armchairs with the same swirling patterned cushions as the divan.

He took one of the armchairs and Sian sat, as she usually did, on the divan. She poured the tea and pushed forward the malt bread and butter and asked, 'How's the work going?'

'It's coming. I'd just started on this when I had the pile-up. I've got to get the feel of it again.'

He was looking around. He would have seen some of the room through the open archway, but he had obviously not been sufficiently interested to walk in during the afternoon. She was sure that no thought of privacy or intrusion would have deterred him. If he had wondered what the room looked like he would have found out.

Now he got up and went to the corner where she sometimes amused herself with some modelling. That wasn't her line at all, and she only dabbled in it because the feel of the clay could be relaxing and therapeutic. She knew that she had no talent there. She hadn't taken modelling at art school. It was only since she had a home of her own that she had bought some modelling clay and made models, and destroyed them and started again, like doodling, or doing crossword puzzles.

She said, 'Don't look at that.'

'Why not? What is it?'

'A cat.' Well, it was as much a cat as anything else. It was squat and sitting and it had two pointed ears. He said, 'Do you sell them in the gallery?' and she gurgled with laughter.

'You're joking! Langley wouldn't touch stuff like that with a long pole. I only do them for amusement.'

'Who gets the laughs?'

'Me! I make them. Then I laugh like a drain and then I roll them up into a ball again.'

'Sounds sadistic.'

'No more than a snowman or a sandcastle. Haven't you ever written anything you've torn up and tossed into a wastepaper basket?'

'Many a time.'

'There you are, then.'

'All right,' he said, 'but don't flatten him while I'm here, will you? He looks a bit like a friend of mine.'

'You must have some funny friends.'

'I do.' He came back and drank his tea, and asked if anything interesting had happened over at the gallery this afternoon.

'Not what you'd call interesting,' she said. 'We sold a few things, and I got on with a miniature I'm painting, and Langley stripped down a couple of chairs he bought this morning.'

She smiled, because although it was dull to Barney it hadn't been dull to Sian, and he said, 'You're fond of Langley, aren't you?'

'Of course.' She was colouring. She tried to hide it, tossing her head a little so that the hair fell across her cheek.

'How fond?'

'Surely that's my business.'

'Are you going to marry him?'

This was direct talk, but you couldn't be offended because Barney was fond of Langley too. It might not be his business, but you couldn't blame him for showing interest. And he didn't sound disapproving. She said, 'We've only known each other three months. It's early days.'

'It's ninety days.'

'So?' she said. 'That might be a long time at the pace you live, but here it's early days.'

He smiled. 'I wish you luck, I think you're the very girl for him.'

He might be laughing at her, although if he was it wasn't blatant, the mockery was under control. She said, deliberately admitting everything, 'I hope Langley thinks so.'

'You don't know how he feels?'

'No.'

Barney Hollis said, 'There are very few things you can't make happen if you put your mind to it.'

She wished that was true. She smiled, 'Like you said, I'm a disbelieving woman, I can't believe that.'

'Care to bet on it?'

She said, slightly wistful, 'What do you do, wish on a wishing bone?'

'Wish on anything, but having made the wish you must follow it through.'

It had been enough for him to wish and to follow, he'd got all he wanted easily enough, and now, even if his work was tough and realistic, he was still a dealer in dreams. She said, 'You may manipulate characters in a play like that, but you can't always do it with flesh and blood.'

'You can, you know.' He put down his cup and leaned forward, a man prepared to argue and prove a theory. 'Take this situation.' He sounded as though she had tossed it in as a theme for his next TV script, and maybe that was the way

34

he was considering it. 'Langley and you. You're interested in him, and speaking as an onlooker you have a great deal in common. I'd be prepared to give you my blessing any day.'

'Thank you,' she murmured, and this time the mockery was hers. He ignored it. He said, 'Langley needs stirring up for his own sake. While he's hesitating you might get another offer or decide to move on.'

She said, 'Neither very likely.'

'Either a possibility, as Langley should realize. And I should think a little competition is the obvious answer to that.'

She waited. Then she sipped her tea. Then she asked, 'Who's competing for what?'

'I'm competing with Langley. For you.'

She sputtered with laughter into her teacup. But he didn't laugh. He said, 'This is serious. This is the way to go about it. If Langley can't see for himself that you're an attractive girl somebody has to spell it out for him.'

In a little way Barney had spelled it out already. Langley hadn't been too happy to find them sharing a joke this morning, and he had been very emphatic about the way girls fell for Barney. She said, 'Well, don't overplay it, but I wouldn't object to you mentioning that I do seem to be a help about the place.'

'And you cook a superlative Victoria sponge.'

'I think he knows that.' She wrinkled her nose. 'Not very glamorous, is it?'

'But nourishing.'

She went on laughing, although somewhere inside her the laughter stopped. Not very glamorous but nourishing, that was Sian Rowan. She said, 'Have some more tea. Have some more of this malt loaf stuff.'

He took both, and as he scooped sugar into the tea he said, 'May I do another hour or so in Nelly's room before I call quits for tonight?'

'It isn't my room. I'm more likely to disturb you than you are to disturb me. I sometimes put the radio on and I walk around a lot, and I have been known to shift furniture, for what there is and what it's worth.'

He grinned. 'That won't disturb me. You should see the kind of places where I usually work.'

'Are they noisy?'

'They can be deafening.'

And full of distractions, no doubt. Like the girl called Natalie. She said, 'Aren't you going to phone Natalie?'

'As soon as I get back.' He meant back to the gallery. George would have let him use this phone, but apparently Natalie would keep until Barney had finished work for the day. Although that might be a compliment to her. Under doctor's orders talking to Natalie might rate as an excitement to be rationed and sparing.

Barney said, 'Would you mind if I took this into the next room and finished it while I work?'

'Of course. Anyhow, I have to sew a curtain to put up.'

'Very symbolic,' said Barney. 'With luck we'll have Langley insisting you put a door you can double lock between us.'

She said gaily, 'Fiona has already offered me one.' But 'Heavens *no*!' Fiona had said at the suggestion that Sian really needed a door.

Sian said, 'Your friend who looks like my cat, what was he in for?'

Barney turned to look again at the little squat hunk of clay. 'In for? Oh, you mean *inside*! No, he's not been in prison, he's a dean of philosophy.'

'Well, well!' said Sian.

She heard the slow soft tapping of the typewriter from Nelly's room as she finished her tea, then she went over to the clay model. It had had a vague sort of face and now she pinched the nose, and made mouth and eyebrows, and sat back on her heels and laughed silently at it.

She wouldn't flatten it, she'd let Barney see it first. Now he'd given it a personality she doubted if she'd ever have the heart to flatten it.

That evening she sewed the curtain, and George put in screws and fixed a curtain rail. The curtain was unbleached linen, and looked effective against the white walls.

Nelly's room was screened off now, although if she ever felt like haunting she could surely slip through a few folds of linen. Sian lay in bed that night and looked at the curtain in the moonlight, smiling at her own little private joke about asking Nell Gwynn how she should go about making Langley Hollis fall in love with her.

Nell hadn't told her, but Barney had, and it could just work. The sort of counsel Nell might have given . . . 'Lawks, sweeting, he's not the only rooster in the woodpile. Show him that a likely-looking wench can have her pick of the . . . whatever was the seventeenth-century term for "talent".'

Sian went on smiling. 'A girl after my own heart' Barney had said of Nell. And talking of competition, Natalie was up against a formidable rival if only she knew it. Nell Gwynn, no less . . .

Langley was downstairs next morning when Sian walked into the kitchen of the Little Gallery. There was no sign of Barney, but Emily was up, of course, and Langley was drinking coffee.

'Good morning,' said Sian. They both said good mornings and, while Emily poured for Sian, Langley said, 'Barney tells us he's working over at the store, using one of the rooms there for an office.'

He sounded as though it had come as a complete surprise and Sian said, 'Didn't you know he used to do that? Write up in Nelly's room?'

'Whose room?' Langley frowned. 'Oh, you mean the storeroom. No, it's the first I've heard of it.'

Over the frying bacon Emily's expression said it was the first she had too, but Fiona had been definite enough and so had George and surely they should know. Sian couldn't throw much light on the matter, nor could she answer Langley's question, 'Why can't he work in his room here?'

She said, 'I don't know. Have you asked him?'

'He says the view's better from the storeroom.'

'Well, it is.' It looked down on the street and out over the housetops. It was quite a little vista because the stores was the only three-storeyed house in the village. Barney's window in this house, as Sian remembered, had a limited range.

Langley said, 'I suppose he knows what he's doing, but it seems an unnecessary fuss when there are rooms here.'

Sian had collected the post off the mat as usual. Now she handed the letters to Langley, he opened them as Emily served breakfast, discussing them with Sian, and she scribbled notes on a couple that needed replies. She would type those out before she did anything else.

Barney came in when the mail was stacked neatly at Sian's elbow and she was half-way through her second and last piece of toast. He offered a general 'Good morning' and reached for the coffee pot.

Langley said, 'We're still trying to work out why you're setting up office down the road.'

Barney poured black coffee, and took several gulps. 'I told you, I like the view.'

He turned his head slowly and looked at Sian over the coffee cup and grinned, and she looked away quickly because the grin caught her unprepared and it was loaded. Langley would have had to be blind not to have read a *double entendre* in that.

She wanted to protest, 'It's nothing to do with me,' but that would only have focused attention on Barney's grin, so she swallowed the rest of her toast in a hurry and said, 'Shall I open the shop? And I've brought the new battery for the bell.'

'Thank you' said Langley.

'See you,' said Barney.

Sian got out and opened the door into the street, replaced the old bell battery, then went into the studio and started on the two letters. She was finishing the first when Langley joined her, and he read it over her shoulder and said thank you when she took it out of the machine and laid it flat for signature.

Barney left after breakfast and didn't return for lunch, and Sian wasn't sorry. She wasn't sure how far his humour might stretch in this affair, and she wasn't adept at play-acting. She had felt quite guilty when Langley said suddenly, mid-morning and without warning, 'Sian, I know there's no need to say this, but don't take anything Barney says too seriously, will you?'

She had mumbled, 'What sort of thing?' and Langley had said, 'Well, he's going to get bored down here, and you're a pretty girl, and—'

She had smiled then and said, 'Am I?'

'Of course you are.'

Now that was progress. He'd never said that before. She had said happily, 'I'm sure girls come a lot prettier where he comes from, and if he said they didn't I wouldn't believe a word of it.'

Langley had looked relieved, and it had made her day. She almost finished the miniature; when it was done she was going to help with the chair upholstering and just before closing time she did one pink spot on the rocking horse.

She said, 'Will it be all right if I paint a spot a day? I don't want to lose him too soon.'

As soon as he was put into the showroom she knew he would be sold, and she was going to miss him. Langley said, 'Take your time,' and she finished the spot dead on half-past five.

As she went through Fiona's floor Fiona called, 'Barney's still there.' 'She tells me tonight,' said Sian. 'Now I've got a curtain up.'

She heard the typewriter through the curtain, and she sat down in an armchair and listened to it for a while. The tapping was halting, but for a man with one arm in a sling it wasn't bad. It made a queer little rhythm, quite soothing in an erratic staccato fashion. When the typing stopped she missed it, and made herself sit up and think about getting tea. She wondered if she should ask Barney if he wanted some.

'Hi there!' he called.

'Yes?' she answered.

'Are you decent? Can I come in?'

'Yes.'

He looked in through the curtain. 'How did the day go?'

'Very well. I've nearly finished a miniature I'm painting, and Langley has warned me about you.'

'That's promising.'

'I think so.'

'Right, now how about coming out for a meal?'

She didn't know about that. She said, 'I haven't washed, or anything.'

'Then wash.'

It hadn't been much of an excuse. She said, 'Where could we go? There's nowhere here, and the bus service is dreadful.'

He explained patiently, 'We ring for a taxi, and we could try the Royal.'

That was a hotel in the nearest town. She said, 'I thought the doctor said no racketing around.'

'You don't call a meal at the Royal racketing around?'

It would be nice. She would enjoy an *haute cuisine* dinner. Although she wouldn't admit it, of course, she had never been taken out to dinner in her life. When she had eaten out it had been with Aunt Mary or one of her few girl-friends. She smiled, 'You look as if you've been in a punch-up. They'll never let you into the Royal.'

He touched the scar on his cheek. 'It makes me look a hard man, we'll get quick service. How long do you need to wash?'

'Half an hour? I can change too in half an hour.'

'Right.' He let the curtain fall again and she heard him go through his own door and close it, and go down the stairs. She wondered if he would tell Langley and thought he would and hoped he would, because then perhaps Langley would ask her out to dinner, or to a theatre, or somewhere.

Anything you wish, Barney had said, if you follow the wish through. She ran for the bathroom, and washed and changed into a sleeveless white dress she had bought from Fiona last week, and wished and wished that her next date would be with Langley.

CHAPTER THREE

SIAN couldn't see the road from her own window, so she went into Nelly's room and stood in the little alcove with its raised dais and looked down and waited.

Half an hour, she had said, and it was half an hour since Barney had said 'Right' and gone off, presumably to wash and change himself and ring a taxi and, she hoped, let Langley know what he was about.

There really was very little doing in this village. From the vantage-point up here she could see the main road end to end and count the people in it on two hands. Of course it was after teatime, the shops were closed, almost everybody was indoors, but she couldn't see Barney Hollis settling for this for long.

When he had said, 'You should be in the kind of places I usually work,' he had sounded nostalgic, as though noise and bustle were part of their charm. She felt the doctors were going to be surprised at his rate of recovery as soon as the inevitable boredom set in.

She saw the taxi coming. It was big, black, and looked a bit like a hearse from up here, which it might well have been as J. Poole and Sons, taxis, were also Jonas Poole and Sons, Undertakers.

She ran downstairs, hearing the television as she passed George and Fiona's living-room. She'd look in on her way back and tell them about her evening out; it would interest Fiona at any rate. She went out by the side door and met Barney coming round to it.

He looked at her approvingly. 'Very nice,' he said.

'Thank you,' she said. 'Fiona's boutique. Don't think Carnaby Street's got it all.'

The taxi was waiting and it wasn't a hearse. It was a car with real leather seats and plenty of leg room, and one of the Poole sons standing by with a huge grin and the door open.

Sian stepped in and slid back on the seat. Barney followed her, settling himself carefully. As the car started she asked, 'How many bones did you break?'

'Not so many as you'd think.' He shifted his left arm, the one in the sling, so that it stood less chance of bumping against the side. 'Mind you, I bent a few.'

You tended to forget that. It seemed impossible while he was still carrying scars, limping and bandaged, but you did forget it, and she said with belated but genuine concern, 'Are you all right? Bouncing about in this great car isn't going to unset anything, is it?'

He grimaced, 'That's a revolting thought to set the mood for a romantic evening!'

He was all right. Anyhow Poole junior was driving carefully, and a car like this had comfortable suspension. She laughed, 'I'll bet this is the first time in your life you've ever been at a real disadvantage. A backhander wouldn't finish you, but it would rock you a bit, wouldn't it?'

She couldn't think of anyone else she knew to whom she wouldn't have been all sympathy at a time like this, and it was his own fault it became a joke. He said reproachfully, 'You have a malicious streak. I'm beginning to wonder if Emily and Langley are mistaken about you. Emily says you're a very considerate girl. Not a selfish bone in your body, Emily says.'

'Does she?' She turned to look out of the window so that he couldn't see her eyes, just the pale pure line of her profile. 'And what does Langley say about me?'

'Nothing recently,' said Barney. 'But when I mentioned you were having dinner with me he stiffened up. I'll be best man at your wedding before I leave here.'

She looked back, smiling. 'And never will the term be more undeserved!'

'That's right,' he agreed. He leaned back in his corner of the taxi, watching her in hers. 'I can see it all; at the village church, you in your long white dress and your long white veil and your sheaf of lilies.'

She wasn't sure how far she should let the laughter go.

Her feelings for Langley were no joke at all, they were completely serious, and in his way Barney was helping because, until he came with his nonsense, Langley had seemed to be unaware of her as anything but an efficient assistant. Now, today, he had said she was a pretty girl. Tomorrow with luck, who knows?

All the same she felt uneasy under Barney Hollis's scrutiny. She said coolly, 'That's right. That's my dream. What's Natalie's?'

He was concerning himself enough in Sian's affairs, so why should he expect reticence for his own? But he only grinned, 'Well, it isn't a long white veil and a sheaf of lilies!'

She hadn't supposed it was. She pried on, 'Are you marrying Natalie?' He'd asked her that about Langley, she didn't care of course whether Barney had marriage plans or not, but she suddenly wanted the discussion off Langley and herself.

'The doctors said no excitement. I don't think they'd allow me Natalie.'

'I didn't mean tomorrow. I meant some time.'

'Even the prospect might be too much.'

He wasn't telling, if there was anything to tell. So she said, 'What's the Royal like inside? I've passed it by, but I've never been in.' And for the rest of the trip -- about fifteen minutes -- Barney described it so that she was expecting something right out of the Barretts of Wimpole Street and it came as a pleasant surprise to find that, although the décor was plush and gilt, the general effect was exhilarating.

She stood in the foyer and smiled up at the huge crystal chandelier and said, 'Now that's what I call beautiful.'

'So's the food,' said Barney. 'That's why we're here.'

No one objected to him looking as though he had been in a recent fight. They were received by a dignified waiter with every appearance of welcome and guided to a table flanked by fluted pillars and backed by a massive mirror in a golden frame.

They were handed large menus and given time to read and ponder and decide. Sian's eyes skimmed the list. This

44

was going to be a meal to remember. She smiled blissfully in anticipation and Barney asked, 'What are you having?'

She said, 'You choose.'

He looked a little surprised, as though the girls he took out to dinner rarely said that. 'Give me a clue,' he said. 'I know my preferences, but I don't know yours.'

She had intended to bluff. She had read enough magazine articles to recognize the dishes for what they were. She could have pretended she ate out like this as often as anybody, but somehow she heard herself saying, 'I'm not sure I do know my preferences. I never really dined out in style before!'

He didn't believe her, and from a girl of twenty-one it took some believing. He said, 'Where have you been, in a convent or a cave?'

'Commuting between a house and a hat shop.' She saw them both again – the little flat and Aunt Mary who had reared her, and who had been loving and ailing and needing so much care; and Madame Hélène's and the daily stream of predictable clients who had come to buy those predictable hats.

Not that she had either Aunt Mary or Mrs. Griggs to blame for the dullness of her own life before she came here. If she had been a less ordinary soul herself she would have had at least the occasional date. Someone would have noticed her and managed to meet her.

She wished she hadn't started this. She put a forefinger on his menu, flat on the table before him and upside down to Sian. 'What's that?' she said. 'How about beginning with that?'

'Apple pie. You're in the wrong section.'

'It could happen to anybody,' she said, and smiled, chin high, and he smiled too. 'Try again,' he said. She checked with her own menu for layout, and then stabbed at his, and the luck of the draw wasn't bad at all.

Iced melon and ginger, lobster thermidor, and apple pie which turned out to be apple strudel and came with a large helping of whipped cream. After the lobster thermidor perhaps it brought the selection down a little on the rich side, but it was delicious, all of it.

Barney left his whipped cream, but Sian didn't. She ate her whole meal.

They talked as they ate, mostly about the gallery and the village. It was six years since Barney had left the village, but the same families, with very few exceptions, were still in the same houses. They talked about Langley's paintings. She said, 'He is good, isn't he?' Barney nodded.

She asked how the play was coming and what it was about. He said, 'At the moment it's fighting back. When I get the upper hand I'll tell you.'

They were on the strudel course and she ate a piece. 'Do that,' she said. She thought – You won't tell me. Except perhaps as an exercise for marshalling your facts, like talking to yourself. Because I'm the same as Emily, I don't understand the kind of people or the kind of living you write about. It would be no help to discuss it with me, I'm a stranger in that land. She said gaily, 'It should be a winner, with Nell Gwynn for your inspiration.'

He raised his glass. 'To Nell.'

Sian raised hers. 'Nell, and other absent friends.'

That meant Langley to her, and surely Natalie to him. She asked, 'Is Natalie pretty? Do you have a picture of her?'

If he carried a photograph he would probably enjoy showing it, but he said, 'No, I don't, and her name's Natalie Wender, and if you watch television next Wednesday you can see her. She's an *au pair* girl who gets caught up in a spy ring.'

'She's an actress?' That was a stupid question. Of course it was in a play. She was hardly likely to be appearing on the news, having unmasked an espionage mastermind.

He said, 'Yes.' And a good actress or she wouldn't get a television role. She asked, 'Is it your play?'

'No, she hasn't been in anything of mine yet.'

But she probably would be some time and that would be nice, like Sian and Langley worked together. He must be

46

proud of Natalie and she of him, like Sian was proud of Langley.

Poole junior was waiting for them in the car park at the appointed hour, and they reached the stores and got out of the taxi here. Barney paid off Poole junior and Sian, putting her key in the keyhole of the side door, heard them guffawing. Perhaps the tip was an extra good one, or they were sharing a joke – if they were she hoped it wasn't at her expense.

Barney joined her as she opened the door, and she asked, 'What's amusing him?'

'I am,' said Barney. 'He doesn't believe I was in a car crash. He thinks I had this coming to me in a dark alley.'

'He does enjoy a joke, doesn't he?' said Sian.

'That he does,' said Barney. 'And as a lad who has to spend most of his working life looking like one of the mourners who's to begrudge him the chance?'

The side entrance led directly on to the stairs if you turned sharp right. If you opened the door immediately ahead it led into the ground floor of the shop. The foyer was so cramped that when they both moved in it wasn't easy to close the outer door again, and Sian stepped backwards up the first step.

Barney closed the door and turned to face her and she was level with him, and he put a hand on her shoulder and said, 'Thank you.'

It was dark down here. There was light at the top of the staircase because that was the floor where George and Fiona lived, and it filtered down so palely that this was a little pit of shadows. She knew that if he kissed her it would mean less than nothing, no more than the hand on her shoulder; all the same she would rather he didn't kiss her. She said, 'Thank *you*, I had a marvellous time. Are you going to see me home?'

'As far as George's living-room, I thought,' he said.

'Now I was thinking of dropping in on Fiona.'

'What could be handier? We'll go together.'

Sian tapped on the living-room door, and Fiona called,

47

'Come in, Sian.' George was in an armchair, Fiona had her feet up on the settee, and the remains of their supper were on a little table before them. They had expected it to be Sian, but they both raised eyebrows at seeing Barney with her, especially when she explained, 'We've been to the Royal, to dinner.'

'What did you have?' Fiona wanted to know.

'Lobster thermidor.'

Fiona sighed, 'Very grand! It makes mousetrap cheese and cream crackers taste a bit thin.' She looked at George, who sighed too and looked at Barney and said, 'I might have known as soon as you got back the quiet life would be over. Now she wants to go to the Royal. I thought you were supposed to be a sick man.'

'So I am,' said Barney. 'Tommy Poole drove us at twenty miles an hour all the way.'

George grinned. He had a thin face that seemed to have more angles than most faces, and made some of his grins look positively devilish. He said, 'I shouldn't have thought you'd have been too comfortable riding behind Tommy, seeing how near you came to following him in your little wooden box.'

'George!' Fiona protested, but George went on grinning and Barney said, 'Not yet, boy, not yet.'

But Barney could have been killed. Sian remembered that George, who had driven Langley to the hospital after that phone call, had looked so bleak that she had hardly recognized him. Langley had been prepared for the worst, Emily had been insisting that it wasn't going to happen, and George had said savagely to nobody in particular, 'He hasn't done half he's going to do. He can't finish like this. If he does there's no sense, there's no bloody reason in anything.'

Now George chuckled. 'You watch it,' he said, 'you're not out of the wood yet. You could well be on borrowed time.' And Fiona said, 'Shut *up*, will you, George? Sian, Barney, have some coffee.' 'Have some brandy,' said George.

Sian envied what was between these three. Barney Hollis

might not have seen George and Fiona for months, but their friendship was easy and without restraint. They took it for granted. It must be good to have friendships you could take for granted.

She sat in the warm room sipping her coffee, feeling part of the affection they shared. She felt they all liked her, and she knew she liked them. George and Barney drank their brandy, and Sian held some knitting wool that Fiona was winding. They watched television in snatches and Barney and George argued about what was good entertainment and what wasn't. 'Do they often go on like this?' Sian asked Fiona, and Fiona said,

'Oh, they do.' She smiled across at them and shook her head. 'Don't men talk some nonsense,' she said.

When Fiona took the tray out to the kitchen Sian went too, and picked up the tea towel as Fiona turned on the tap. Fiona said, 'You know, I thought it was Langley. I've said to George that I was sure you and Langley were made for each other.'

Fiona had a sweet, almost beautiful face, and ash-brown hair waving softly, and when Sian said, 'It is Langley,' she looked puzzled.

Sian took the first cup and polished it as though it was going on display. 'Barney just asked me out for a meal. It doesn't mean—' she shrugged, 'you know – well, I'm not Barney's type, am I? And he certainly isn't mine, and – well, he isn't Langley, is he?'

Fiona whisked the suds enthusiastically with her little mop and agreed that Barney wasn't Langley. 'George and I are fond of Barney,' she said. 'I suppose he's George's best friend, but there's no denying he's the wild one. Langley's the sort of man who'd mean what he was saying to a girl, but I'm fairly sure that Barney wouldn't. I think it could be out of sight out of mind with Barney.'

Sian found Fiona's concern for her so touching that she said, 'This is going to sound silly, but since Barney came Langley has started to worry about me. I suppose he knows Barney too, and if Langley doesn't want me hurt I figure that's something, don't you?'

Fiona laughed, 'It's a start. Does he know where you've been tonight?'

'Yes. Barney told him we were going.'

Fiona looked happier. 'I'm glad about that,' she said. 'I'm glad it's Langley. You're so right for each other, you two.'

'I think so,' said Sian. 'I hope so.'

They finished washing up and went back to the living-room where Barney and George were now arguing party politics. Sian just put her head in to say 'Good night,' and then ran up to her own room because it was plenty late enough for bed.

She had enjoyed herself immensely, it had been a very good evening. She carried the glow of it with her, and smiled at the little clay figure squatting on the shelf, 'Hello, you ugly little man.' Barney hadn't seen him with his face. His friend, the dean of philosophy with the pointed ears.

She picked him up. She'd sit him beside Barney's type-writer in Nelly's room and he could welcome Barney in the morning. Then she put him down again, because she had another idea that seemed in her elevated mood something of an inspiration. She took off her nice white dress, picked up another lump of modelling clay from its plastic bag, and began to work on another head.

She sang as she worked. She had no voice at all, but she was having fun and she sang little snatches of this and that, as she pinched and pummelled. She loved the feel of the clay, the way it resisted and then became pliable beneath her fingers. Her hands, covered in it, seemed like someone else's hands, and when she was satisfied that this would do she was appalled to realize how late it was. A joke was a joke, but spending half the night on it was ridiculous. Anyhow, it did look like Barney. It was craggy and near Neolithic, but when he saw it he'd know who it was.

It was also heavy. She carried it slowly and carefully into his room and set it down on the table, then she took a piece of paper from the pile and one of the ball-point pens and wrote, 'A small thank-you for a delicious evening.'

Of course Fiona and George had been long in bed and asleep, and creeping to the bathroom Sian wondered how she would explain herself if they had seen her, in bra and pants, hands spooky-white with modelling clay, at half past two in the morning.

Inevitably next morning she overslept and went rushing into the gallery ten minutes late. Someone had already picked up the mail, and both Barney and Langley were in the kitchen having breakfast.

Sian paused in the doorway, breathing fast, to apologize, 'I'm late, I'm sorry.'

Langley said quietly, 'Only a few minutes.'

'Oversleep?' said Barney.

'I – suppose so.' She sat down and looked at the mail, spread out around Langley. 'Anything interesting?'

'An auction,' he said, and handed her the catalogue. 'And someone wants to know if we've got a model of Dr. Palmer the Poisoner in Staffordshire ware.'

'Have you?' asked Barney with interest.

'No,' said Sian. 'But we've got Robbie Burns and Jenny Lind. I wonder if they'd settle for either of them.'

'I shouldn't think so,' said Barney.

Langley had finished his breakfast and Sian didn't want any, so that when Langley stood up she did too. Emily said, 'Aren't you going to have any toast?' and Sian said, 'No, thanks,' and Emily said, 'I don't know,' as though she wasn't too pleased about something.

Sian wondered how much Barney had told them this morning about last night, because as soon as they reached the studio Langley asked, 'Did you have a pleasant evening?'

'Very, thank you,' Sian said brightly.

She went to her working corner and looked down at the miniature. She'd finish that today, then it could be framed and posted and Melinda Ann's grandmother would have her birthday present.

Behind her Langley said a little hesitantly, 'Sian, would you have dinner with me?'

No, he wasn't like Barney. With Langley it was a real date. Something special, nothing casual about it. He asked as though a refusal would hurt, and of course she wasn't going to refuse. She said, 'I'd love to.'

'Tonight?'

'Yes, yes.' Thank you, Barney, and I can play my own hand from here . . .

'Where would you like to go?' Langley asked.

Not the Royal again, not twice in two nights. She said, 'What about the Chinese place? Do you like Chinese food?'

She had been there once for lunch, when Langley had given her a day off to do some shopping and she and Emily had gone to town. Now Langley said, 'Fine, I'll collect you about half past seven?'

She nodded, and Barney strolled in. She was glad he hadn't come sooner, and she wished he would go. But instead he walked across, and as she picked up her paint brush he leaned over her shoulder and looked at the miniature and the photograph beside it.

'Very neat,' he said. 'You'd have made a good forger.'

She said, 'I must remember, that might come in handy some day.'

He watched her make a couple of almost invisible strokes, then she said, 'Hadn't you better be getting on with your play?'

'Why? Do I make you nervous?'

'Of course not. Although I don't know – I half expect you to jolt my elbow.'

Langley said, 'We are working in here, Barney.'

'So I see,' said Barney. He circled the rocking horse. 'Can I paint a few spots?'

'No,' said Sian, 'I'm rationing him to one spot a day, I want him to last.'

'You should have him ready for the Christmas rush,' said Barney. He patted the wooden head. 'Find him a good home,' he said. 'He's a splendid beast.'

The doorbell rang as he went out and Langley asked Sian, 'How is the play going?'

'I don't know, he hasn't talked to me about it.'

She went on painting. Langley said, 'I must finish that picture.' He meant Deniston Crag, and he looked at the chairs he had to upholster, and Sian urged, 'Do some painting now, the chairs can wait.'

But it turned into a busy morning, so that neither of them got much work done in the studio. The man who wanted Dr. Palmer in pottery rang up, and Langley spent some time phoning possible sources of supply.

In 1856 when they'd hanged the good doctor in front of Stafford jail his effigy would have been obtainable in fairs and markets all over the country for a few pence, but now he was a collectors' piece, and the best Langley was offered at the end of a morning of phone calls was one chipped specimen without a nose.

Sian served several customers, and when the phone rang just before lunchtime she thought it might be Dr. Palmer again. Langley answered in the studio. Sian was showing a secret drawer in a rosewood workbox to a woman who looked as though she might buy, and she wasn't pleased when Langley came out to say it was Barney wanting to speak to her.

'What's he want?' she muttered.

Langley said he didn't know, but the spell of the secret drawer was broken. The customer was looking across at another and cheaper workbox and saying, 'That's pretty too. How much is that?' and Langley told her and brought it over for her to compare, and Sian went into the studio to pick up the telephone.

She said, 'What do you want?'

'Is the shop shut?'

'No, it isn't, and I'd got a customer in.'

'All right,' he said. 'Nip back to your customer, then nip over here, will you?'

'What for?'

'I want to talk to you.' He put down the phone. It was George's business line and perhaps Barney felt it shouldn't be commandeered a moment longer than necessary. Or perhaps he thought Sian's customer was fuming.

Either would be preferable to the possibility that he considered he had made his point, and 'I want to talk to you' was enough to have her haring over at the first opportunity.

She listened to the dialling tone for a few seconds, then she put the phone on its cradle and went back into the display room. Her customer was leaving, smiling as she went, and Langley was thanking her.

Sian said, 'That was quick.'

'She's thinking about it. She can't make up her mind which she wants.'

Which meant she would almost certainly decide to buy something else somewhere else. Sian said regretfully, 'She was hooked on that workbox. She'd practically got her old love letters in the secret drawer.'

'What did Barney want?' Langley asked.

'He wants me to go over.'

'Why?' He was both curious and slightly annoyed, and she shook her head. 'I don't know. He thought the gallery was closed for lunch.'

'Did you say you'd have lunch over there with him?'

'I don't think so.' She was sure she hadn't. She said with some impatience herself, 'I suppose I'd better see what he wants. I'll be right back.'

It was only a couple of minutes away, easier than the trouble of dialling the number, and it just might be important. As she hurried along the road she realized that she was hopping to Barney's whims as fast as any of them, but he needn't think she'd do it often.

She let herself in by the side door, and paused for a moment on her way up to look into the kitchen where Fiona was heating a tin of soup. Fiona and George had a light snack at lunch time, closing the shop for half an hour; George would be up any minute.

Sian said, 'I can't stop, I just wanted to tell you Langley's taking me to the Chinese restaurant tonight – the Lotus Bough or whatever it's called.'

'Splendid,' said Fiona. 'Things are moving.'

54

Sian certainly was. She ran up the second flight of stairs, and opened the storeroom door. Barney was at the window, typing away with his good hand, and she said, 'What do you want? What's it all about?'

'That,' said Barney. He pointed to the clay head she had modelled last night and perched on the end of his table. 'Would you mind shifting it?'

It did take up some room and with an arm in a sling he obviously hadn't been able to move it himself, but George or Fiona would have helped, there had been no need to bring Sian over. She said huffily, 'Oh, push it off. It's not that heavy, it won't crash through the floor.'

'Don't be stupid,' he said. 'I don't want it smashed. Just get it down for me, will you?'

She put it on the floor, and he said, 'Thanks.' He sat looking at it. He asked, 'When did you do it?'

'Last night, after I came up.'

'It's good.'

'It was a joke.'

He grinned. 'So I should hope if it's supposed to be me! But you've got to get down to some serious work.'

She stared at him. 'You mean – this sort? It's amateurish, it's – childish.'

'It's like the work of no child I'd care to meet,' he said. 'Those photographs you're copying, they're neat and they're pretty, but no one's going to stop in their tracks to look at them. This thing has impact. You've got power here, and no comfortable little talent.'

She said, 'You're fooling.'

'No.'

'But how would you know?' She wasn't sure she wanted him to know. It was something to accept your limitations, to be content and safe. To open a door might let in a whirlwind.

He said, 'You know it yourself.'

'I *don't!*' She looked down at her hands and remembered the wet clay on them. She said, 'I only do it to amuse myself. I gave your friend a face.'

55

'Show me.' He got up and went ahead of her through the curtain into her room. She babbled, 'Is it like him? Does he look like that?'

She wanted Barney to laugh, but he didn't laugh. He said, 'You've got a good light here, the makings of an adequate studio.'

'Look,' she protested, 'I *work* in a studio, over at the gallery.'

'Can you see yourself doing this in there?'

'Well, no.'

'So it's got to be here.'

She said 'Why?' and his voice was almost gentle. 'Because copyists are two a penny. Keep those hands of yours chained to that, and one day I hope they strangle you.'

She felt he could have put that less graphically. It was flattering of course to be told you had a talent you hadn't suspected, and she enjoyed playing about with clay and there was no reason why she shouldn't do more. She said, 'Very well. I don't think anybody's going to be stopped in their tracks by anything I've knocked together, but all right, I'll sculpt on, and thank you for your kind encouragement.'

He turned and looked at her, and it wasn't funny. It was as though she had opened a dark door and couldn't close it, and would never be able to close it again.

He said, 'A dozen or so pieces and we'll have an exhibition at the gallery.'

Set against the delicate workmanship of the kind of thing they sold in the gallery an exhibition of Sian's modelling would have been wildly incongruous, but Barney was talking as though it was as good as done, and she wailed, 'When are you going back?'

'Give me a chance, I've only been here a couple of days.'

And he had. The day before yesterday he had limped into the gallery, and since then he had organized not only her love life but her working life as well. She said, 'That's what I mean. You get things moving too fast.'

He said cheerfully, 'We wouldn't be referring to Langley, would we? What went on after I left this morning?'

Her lips curved. 'He's taking me out to dinner tonight.'

'And that's moving too fast? It seems an obvious follow-up on last night at the Royal to me.'

'We are not talking about Langley. We're talking about the idea of me having an exhibition of this kind of stuff. The gallery has a reputation.'

'For Jenny Lind and Deniston Crag.'

That stung her. She had suspected that Barney didn't really admire Langley's work. It wasn't surprising, but it brought out all her partisanship on Langley's side. She said, 'Deniston Crag is a beautiful picture. All Langley's pictures are beautiful. He's really an artist, not just a craftsman or a word-hack, he is an artist. But maybe you wouldn't understand that, and I've got to get back.'

She turned towards the door, and Barney stood slightly in her way, and as she brushed by he said, 'Don't shove, my balance isn't too good.'

She had shoved a little. She said impatiently, 'It's your own fault I keep forgetting. Why can't you stop sounding so darned healthy?'

Somebody rapped on the door and she called, 'Come in!' It was Langley, and Barney said laconically, 'Manners Makyth Man, but in the circumstances I wouldn't have stopped to knock.'

Langley frowned slightly and Sian scowled. It was ridiculous to pretend there was any real rivalry between Langley and Barney over her. She said, 'I was just coming.'

'Good,' said Langley. 'Emily's got the meal ready. Was it anything important?' He looked at Barney and Barney said,

'Come and look at this.'

Back again into Nelly's room where Barney's head stood on the floor beside the table. Barney said, 'Sian did it.'

Sian wished she hadn't, and she wished that Barney had put her note into the wastepaper basket instead of leaving it there at the edge of the table reading 'Thank you for a delicious evening.'

She wanted to explain, 'I was talking about the food,' but Langley was looking at the head. He said, 'It's you. When did you do it?' The recognition for Barney and the question for Sian.

She said, 'Last night, from memory.' She seemed to be saying this like a loop recording. 'It was a joke.'

Barney said, 'I've been telling her she must do some more, and we must have an exhibition of them at the gallery.'

Sian gave a squeal of protest, and apology. 'Oh, please, I don't know . . .'

'I don't know either,' said Langley. 'It isn't quite the kind of thing our customers expect.'

'Then they'll have a surprise, won't they?' said Barney.

Barney owned half the gallery and took half the profits, but when Sian had said it was time he did something for his money she hadn't wanted this kind of interference. Langley knew best here, and she was embarrassed at the position she found herself in. She explained firmly, 'This isn't my idea, and I don't think it's a very good one.'

Barney said, 'Run along, children, we'll discuss it later,' and when Sian stood undecided he sat down in his chair, switched on the recorder, and picked up the little hand mike.

Langley said, 'All right, we'll talk about it later.'

He drew Sian away and she went, looking back resentfully over her shoulder. She wondered if Barney was amusing himself. Filling the gallery with something that would jolt the clientele might make his enforced stay here less boring.

She wished she hadn't made the wretched head in the first place. And she was beginning to wish that she had been less naïve in admitting how she felt about Langley. She'd taken a chance there. If Barney talked about that he could make her sound such an idiot, and a man as reserved and sensitive as Langley would never understand.

She said, 'Of course we can't put on an exhibition of the stuff. It isn't worth exhibiting.'

They went down the narrow stairs single file. The store had closed for the lunchtime half-hour, George had let Langley in, and now they made for the side door. Two stairs ahead of her Langley said, 'I didn't know you went in for modelling.'

'It's a hobby, hardly that.'

'Yes, well, we'll see, shall we?' On the ground floor he opened the side door and waited for her to step out, then closed it, self-locking, behind them. He smiled at her. 'I can see Barney might like it, but it isn't exactly my taste.'

'Nor mine,' she assured him.

They hurried back and Emily was waiting, looking martyred. Not only was lunch congealing by the minute but, adding insult, there had been a phone call for Langley from someone who wanted ringing back. Emily had two plates in the oven: grilled plaice and a white sauce with a skin on it. She set one plate in front of Sian and one in Langley's place. As Langley went to the telephone Sian said meekly, 'Thank you, Emily.'

'What did Barney want you for?' Emily seemed as curious as Langley had been and Sian said, 'He wanted to talk about a model I made.'

'Did he?' Emily didn't think much of that for a tale. She leaned forward, over the remains of her own meal, and dropped her voice to a confiding level. 'You take a bit of advice from me,' she said. 'You settle for Langley.'

Sian would be delighted to, given the chance.

'Every time,' said Emily. She waved an admonitory fork. 'And don't let Barney turn your head with a lot of nonsense, because he'll be up and off as soon as he's over this little setback, and goodness knows when anybody down here'll see him again.'

'Till the next time he needs you,' said Sian; and Emily smiled wryly. 'And that doesn't come around often, so you settle for Langley.'

'I had the same advice from Fiona.'

'You'll get the same advice from anyone round here,' said Emily.

Langley came back into the kitchen and she turned on him. 'Don't tell me you're actually going to sit down and eat your meal now!'

He sat and smiled across at her. 'Sorry, Emily,' he said. 'Anyhow, it looks very nice.'

Emily sniffed. 'It was very nice – half an hour ago.'

During the afternoon Sian finished Melinda Ann, and framed her in her blue forget-me-nots. She hoped Grandmother would be happy with her birthday present. As Barney said, it was neatly done and pretty. She packed it carefully, addressed it, and tied the final string taut and strong.

The post office was the paper shop, next door to the butcher's and just across the road. She could catch the last post, and she said to Langley, 'I'll just get rid of this.'

'Good,' he said. 'You made an excellent job of it.' ... 'Copy work,' Barney had said. 'Copyists are two a penny.'

She put Melinda Ann on the scales, and the postmistress said she saw Barney was back, and he didn't look so bad after all. 'He doesn't, does he?' said Sian. She would go on with the modelling, she decided, not because Barney had said she should but because she wanted to, but of course there would be no question of putting it on show in the gallery.

A woman crossed the road in front of her, carrying a heavy shopping basket. Her head was bowed and her shoulders stooped as though she bore the weight of the world. Fatigue was in every line of the slowly moving figure, and Sian thought, I could show that so easily; I could catch the shape of weariness there.

On the pavement the woman turned and saw Sian and said 'Hello.' She was a housewife with four children who had just finished the week's wash, and she smiled and said it was a nice day, then went on her way with no idea at all that Sian was visualizing her as the shape of weariness.

When Sian finished at the gallery that night and said good-bye to Langley it was wonderful to have him say, 'You won't forget? Half seven!'

'I won't forget,' she said.

She ran for the stores, and went into Fiona's dress section where a customer was going through the skirt rail while her friend held up the blouse she had just bought and was trying to match. Fiona stood around, ready to give a casting vote if one was needed, and Sian said, 'I like your blouse,' as she made for the dresses.

'Nice, isn't it?' said the girl, holding it.

Fiona's dress selection was, of necessity, limited; but less than you would expect in a village shop, because she had a natural flair for fashion and tended to overstock. Sian found a couple that would see her through tonight's date: a pink scoop-necked gingham, and a short-sleeved angora, light as thistledown and the colour of harebells. She wanted the angora, but it cost five pounds more, so she draped the two over the dress rail and stood back and tried to sell herself the gingham.

The women who had been buying the skirt joined her. They had got what they wanted, and they knew Sian, and they came to see what she was buying. They were particularly interested today because every woman in the village had heard by now that she had been to the Royal with Barney Hollis last night. Tommy Poole's wife had launched that snippet.

After it got around, and it certainly would, that tonight she was out with Langley, they would be watching her like hawks, scared of missing a move. For the moment the fact that she was buying herself a new dress was something to pass on.

They looked at the two dresses, and one of them stroked the angora and said longingly, 'That's the one I'd have.'

Sian nodded. It was the one she was having – the gingham had never stood a chance – and when she put it on, alone in her own room, her hair brushed and her make-up done and her eyes bigger and brighter than she could ever remember seeing them before, she knew the five pounds extra had been money well spent.

Barney had gone when she came in from work, the dress

over her arm. She heard no typewriter, and no voice dictating, and she looked into Nelly's room, to tell him firmly that there was going to be no exhibition in the gallery, but there had been no Barney.

It didn't matter, she could tell him tomorrow. It was nearly six o'clock now and she intended spending the next hour and a half getting ready for her date with Langley.

She was ready long before half past seven, but she wanted to sit and wait and dream, and she was glad Barney had gone. She could do without the tapping typewriter tonight, and certainly without Barney Hollis. She found some music on the radio, and closed her eyes and drifted with it on a cloud with spangled edges. She was in love, and tonight for the very first time she and Langley would be together with no phone ringing, no customers pottering. They could talk and laugh, and swap dreams and memories. Not that Sian had many memories to swap, but she had a host of dreams.

Anyhow, she didn't want to talk about herself. She wanted to listen to Langley, sit there, listening to him, looking at him. It was going to be a blissful evening, and she would have hated herself if she'd settled for the gingham dress.

She saw the car from the window of Nelly's room, just as she had spotted Barney in Poole and Sons' black limousine last night. But that was the only point of similarity between last night and this. Last night was fun and meant nothing. Tonight had her so dizzy with delight before it even started that as she jumped off the dais to get out of the storeroom and down the stairs she nearly fell over that darned head. It was where she had put it at lunch time, and she had to do a quick side-step to avoid going sprawling. She grimaced at it, and it grimaced back, and as a grotesque it was a very good likeness.

She reached the side door before Langley did, and explained, 'I saw you from my window.' She was glad again about the dress, because Langley looked at her as though this was the transformation scene in Cinderella. Then he said, 'You're looking very beautiful.'

The Lotus Bough was in the high street, the entrance door set between two bay windows, a narrow frill of awning running along the top. Parking facilities weren't good. They had to drive around awhile before they found a spot near enough, and then it meant working themselves in between two other cars. But they did park, and as they were booked for eight o'clock they were in easy time. They settled in their table, chose their dinner, and talked about the gallery and Langley's paintings.

Sian said, 'I think, no matter what, you should spend so much time each day painting, just painting. That's important, isn't it? That's your real work.'

It was, Langley admitted; and she knew that this was what she wanted to do with her life, to help Langley who was a real artist. She wanted to look after him as she had looked after Aunt Mary, to keep the worries away from him and leave him free for the creative and splendid things.

She said, 'Why can't we put on an exhibition of your work? A dozen or so. Maybe people would lend you the ones you've sold already, and you could finish Deniston Crag and—'

Langley's expression stilled like a film stopped. He was looking beyond her and she turned and saw the man coming in through the door. He came towards them, the smiling Chinese waiter at his heels.

It was Barney. He stopped at their table and did a double-take, then smiled on them like a benevolent bishop and said, 'Well now, this is a pleasant surprise.'

CHAPTER FOUR

IT was no surprise. Not to Barney. It was a surprise to Langley who was looking annoyed, but made no verbal protest when Barney said 'May I?' and took a chair from the next table and drew it up to join them.

It was a surprise to Sian that almost had her gibbering with rage. Her 'What are you doing here?' came out on a high wavering note.

'Getting a meal,' said Barney.

'Why here?' She had her voice under control again now, tart but under control, and Barney said, 'I like Chinese food. It's a small world, isn't it?'

He picked up his menu and leaned across to consult Sian. 'What are you two having?' She saw the note, held by his thumb, and read, 'Don't be thick, love. If I fancied you I wouldn't give any man the break of a candlelit dinner for two.' There were no candles, there were little fat lamps with red shades. If Langley saw the note she'd never be able to explain it. She said furiously, 'Menu B.'

'B again, please,' said Barney to the waiter.

Langley sighed and Sian said, 'You should be resting. Two nights on the town on the run can't be good for you in your state. You look terrible.'

She presumed Tommy Poole had taxied him again, gently in the roomy limousine, and wondered how he had heard about this. Not from Fiona, but he might have overheard this morning when Langley was asking her.

She would have given a good deal for the chance to say exactly what she thought, but how could she without admitting to Langley that she had practically asked for Barney's help in the first place. Playing a mock admirer off against one that she wanted with all her heart to be for real.

She felt bitter enough for weeping, tears of disappointment and frustration were burning her eyes. She looked at Barney and said again, 'You look terrible.'

He nodded. 'But I always did. Langley got the looks in our family.'

'And you got the gall,' she said. 'Sheer and unadulterated. Go home!'

Barney shrugged, then he half rose, swayed a little and sat down again. Langley said, 'Are you all right?'

'Of course I am. I'll ask our friend here to get me a taxi.'

Langley said, 'Sian, do we let him stay?'

It was his own fault if he took no notice of doctor's orders, but Langley and Emily would have the trouble if he did crack up. It would be too ridiculous to insist he moved to another table, and anyhow his eyes on her would spoil her evening, so feed him for goodness' sake and then send him home – although she suspected Langley would be taking him.

She said, 'Don't ask me, I don't know why you came down here. You couldn't have led a much more hectic life in London.'

He said dryly, 'You've got to be joking.' So he was bored already, and resenting inaction, and she was unsure now what he might do next. She sat through the meal feeling like someone on a powder keg, but there were no fireworks. The food was more exotic and there was no Emily, otherwise they might as well have been in the kitchen at the Little Gallery.

They talked as they had done over meals they had shared there, no chance for confidences or compliments, fair shares in the conversation all round, and when the meal was over they all stood up together.

Barney took the bill and Langley said, 'We'll settle later.' They obviously would. Sian wished she could have snapped, 'So will I, I insist on going dutch,' but that would have sounded too petty.

And it was pouring with rain. When they came in the night had been mild and mellow, and now rain was spattering spitefully on the pavements. Langley said, 'I'll get the car, wait here,' and strode off into the rain, and Sian and Barney stood, sheltering between the windows, under the little striped awning.

She watched Langley going down the street. Without looking at Barney she demanded, 'What are you playing at? Why did you have to turn up here?'

'You want realism, don't you? If I'm supposed to have fallen for you on sight I wouldn't be giving up already, would I? Don't worry,' as Sian fumed, still watching Langley's back, 'Langley's going to win in the end, and the moment he puts the ring on your finger I shall acknowledge defeat and you'll both have a brother for life.'

She turned to glare at him. 'Don't play for laughs, my lad,' she said. 'There may not be much action in this particular backwater, but wait for your girl-friend on television, and don't try to get your entertainment out of the natives.'

'You surprise me more all the time,' said Barney. 'Everyone keeps telling me you're a gentle girl.'

She was a gentle girl, but the reflection she glimpsed in the window of the Lotus Bough looked so ungentle right now that she recognized the dress before the face.

Barney got out of the car in front of the Little Gallery and Sian said to Langley, 'Do come and have some coffee.'

'Thank you,' said Langley. He stopped again in front of the stores and they got out. He said, 'I'm sorry about that. It certainly wasn't the evening I'd hoped for.'

'It wasn't exactly what I was expecting.' They smiled at each other in the lamplight, then went in through the side door and up all the stairs. Reaching the floor under the eaves, with Sian's room and Nelly's room, Sian opened her door and switched on the lights.

Langley had only been in here once before, at lunch time, and now he looked around and said it all looked very charming. She said, 'I'll have coffee in two minutes, do make yourself comfortable.'

She fled down to the kitchen and boiled her kettle, and spooned in her coffee grains, and was back upstairs with it while Langley was still looking at a row of tin trays propped up along a shelf behind the divan.

He said they were colourful, and they were, that was why they were there. They had cost five shillings each from George's hardware section and they were colourful.

She poured the coffee and apologized for its being instant, and he sipped it and said it was very good. This was better. Alone at last. Langley said, 'You didn't tell him where we were going?'

'No.' She had said, 'Langley's taking me out to dinner,' but she hadn't said where. She stressed her denial. 'Of *course* not. Although even if I had done I wouldn't have expected him to turn up as well.'

'I would,' said Langley. 'He finds you attractive.' He looked worried. 'And you don't dislike him, do you?'

She had disliked him tonight. She said, 'The attraction about me is that I'm here and I'm unattached.' She smiled. 'But I'm not an idiot, I wouldn't take anything Barney said seriously.'

'Don't,' said Langley, 'please don't.' He put down his coffee cup and reached for her hand, and her fingers curled at his touch. 'Barney's always thought of life as a joke. For him it always has been.'

There was much unspoken behind those words. Long years of taking and giving. Langley said quietly, 'I know it's a habit, but I still feel responsible for him, and I couldn't bear it if you got hurt.'

'I won't.' She leaned forward, promising fervently, 'I think he's amusing, and that's all I think about him. Anyone who's selfish enough can be carefree and it has a charm, but not for me.'

It was a lovely end to the evening. They drank their coffee and talked about Langley's exhibition. He told her about their father, Barney's and his, and she wished again that she could have known him because he must have been a marvellous man. He had been like Langley, Emily said so. Several times at something Langley said or did Emily had said affectionately, 'Ah, you're just like your father.' Something nice, something kind.

Sian talked a little about Aunt Mary, and they were never again going to be just two people who worked together. Not that they had been only that, they had been friends from the beginning, but tonight it was warmer and closer, and when it was time for Langley to leave he took her in his arms and said, 'You're a very special person, Sian.'

He kissed her, and she thought with absolute assurance, he was waiting for me here from the first moment I breathed. My life was mapped from then. This couldn't be more right and more wonderful. . . .

She woke next morning to a tapping typewriter, and sat bolt upright, her mind whirling with panic. She'd overslept again, and no half measures this time. The sun was pouring in through the window, and if Barney was at work it had to be late.

She grabbed the housecoat beside the divan, and stuck her head through the curtain. 'What time is it?'

'A quarter to ten,' he said. 'And Sunday.'

Of course it was Sunday. She knew it was Sunday. She was going out with Langley this afternoon. 'Oh!' she said. 'Sorry! And sorry I broke in on your work.' She remembered more. 'No, I'm not sorry – you spoiled my date last night!'

'Did I?' He sounded surprised. 'I thought I was helping. Didn't Langley ask you to marry him when you got back here?'

'Of course not.' Not on a first date, not like that.

'All right,' said Barney, 'tell him I did, and see what happens.'

'Ha!' said Sian, 'and he talks about realism. Who's going to believe that? Langley isn't, for one, he knows you too well.'

'He does?'

'Oh, he *does*.' So did Sian. She said accusingly, 'You do think life's a joke, don't you? You don't take anything seriously.'

'Of course it's a joke, ' said Barney. 'The state the world's in today it's got to be a joke.'

She was happy, the world wasn't so bad. She begged, 'Well, please don't interfere any more. Please.'

He tapped another half dozen keys. 'All right, you're on your own.'

'Good,' she said, 'that's good.' He went on tapping, his head bent. Langley had brown hair. When he'd kissed her last night she had run her fingers through it and it had been soft. Barney's hair was black and thick, and it didn't look soft. He looked up from the typewriter.

'Yes,' he said.

He should know if it was good on your own, that was the way he had chosen. She wondered if it was still the way or if Natalie had changed things. She stepped back into her own room, letting the curtain fall behind her, and thought how splendid it was that it was Sunday.

Sian had her Sunday lunch with Fiona and George, usually helping to prepare it, or giving George a hand swabbing the shop floors down while Fiona did the kitchen chores. She went down to the kitchen now, where Fiona and George were having a leisurely breakfast and reading the papers.

Sian had tea and toast with them, and Fiona, basking in the sunshine streaming through the kitchen window, said, 'It's going to be too hot for a cooked meal. How about opening that tinned chicken and throwing a salad together?'

'Perfect,' said Sian. George agreed about the heat. He thought he'd leave the floor cleaning till later, and Sian said, 'If you change your mind, or either of you think of anything I could help with, give me a yell. I'm going to try to do some modelling.'

'That sounds interesting,' said Fiona. 'What are you going to model?'

'Probably nothing,' said Sian. 'I don't think I'm going to be much good at it.'

She put on an old overall and rolled up her sleeves and borrowed an empty packing case from the landing to use as a base. She could hear the typewriter, and the hum of traffic from the road below. If she strained she could hear the radio, and George and Fiona moving around, but after a while she heard nothing. She couldn't have said when the tempo changed, but somewhere as she worked an urgency took over, as though there was something inside the clay clamouring to be freed. It wasn't easy any more. She was impatient, angry when it wasn't right, and wasn't coming right, and never would be right.

It was no good, she couldn't get the shape she needed, but she worked on, and when Fiona came in she was kneeling on the floor, looking hopelessly at it, and didn't hear anyone until Fiona said, 'What on earth's that?'

Fiona held a cup of coffee. She said, 'Morning break. What's it supposed to be?'

'You may well ask,' said Sian. 'I'm not going to ask if you like it.'

'I don't think I do,' said Fiona, and she shivered in the sunshine.

Sian said thank you for the coffee. She heard the type-writer now and Fiona said, 'I just took Barney one in, he looked at me as though I was from another world too. Dinner at two o'clock; all right?'

'Please,' said Sian. But she ate in her room. Fiona brought it up and said, 'It's nearly half past two, so I thought you must still be working.' She took another look at Sian's effort and said, 'I don't think it's growing on me. It makes me feel so lonely.'

'Why?' Sian wondered. Fiona shook her head,

'I don't know. It's a figure, of course, I can see that. It's a woman. But somehow it makes me remember a rock that stood on a hill. There was nothing else, just this rock, and it was high up and sometimes when I was a child I used to think how heavy the sky must be for it.'

She went downstairs and said to George, 'I don't know what Sian's modelling, but I don't think Langley's going to like it. It doesn't look his sort of thing at all.'

Langley didn't see it, but that was no thanks to Sian. She couldn't believe it when Langley tapped on the door and asked if he could come in. She hadn't changed, she had had no idea how time was flying, which showed she hadn't the sense she was born with, or she would have remembered what happened when she made that head of Barney and been prepared for the odd hour or two getting away.

She threw a damp cloth over the figure, opened the door and stepped out and said, 'I am sorry, my watch stopped' – better a white lie than admit she had been so engrossed in a lump of clay she had forgotten him. She said beguilingly, 'Could you go and talk to Barney, I think he's still there.' He wasn't typing, but he might still be there. 'Or George or Fiona. Or wander round the store or something. I won't be ten minutes.'

Langley looked in the storeroom and Barney looked back with no welcome, so then he went downstairs and found George again, and sat with him in the living-room, discussing last week's turnover in their respective businesses until Sian came. She had washed and changed in a commendably short time, and looked none the worse for the hurry. In fact it had put colour in her cheeks. She apologized all over again, and Langley said she had done wonders in ten minutes.

They said good-bye to George, and to Fiona who was down in the sweets section, getting herself a Sunday-afternoon supply of acid and aniseed drops. Then they drove out even further into the country, through wooded lanes, past farms, and over hump-backed bridges. They had tea in a cottage with a thatched roof: hot scones and home-made damson jam so overboiled they had to carve it. They stopped in one village and went round the birthplace of a poet. Sian had heard of him, but couldn't have given a line of his writings to save her life. Langley could. He knew the lot, and as they drove back home he quoted some of the poems.

He had a feeling for the music of the words and a good speaking voice, and she enjoyed listening to him. Nature had been the poet's pet subject, and Langley's paintings were all of the countryside, so she wasn't surprised to hear that the poet had always been something of an inspiration to

Langley. She wondered if he knew that Barney's first inspiration was Nell Gwynn, and thought he probably didn't and decided not to tell him. A flippant note could have spoiled the mood of a romantic afternoon.

They got back to their own village around seven o'clock, and Sian said she wouldn't go back to the gallery, thank you, she had a few things to do at home. She said good-bye to Langley, and closed the door behind her in her own little room like someone with a secret lover.

She did peer through the curtain, glad to see that Barney had gone. She didn't want him asking all about the afternoon, and she didn't want him watching her working, him or anyone. She wasted all the rest of the evening on it. It was a waste of time, she knew that, but it was her own time.

Barney kept his word for the next two days. He didn't interfere in anything. He was working, and he bothered none of them. He had breakfast before he left home, waited till Sian arrived, then went over to Nelly's room, and worked there until around the time the gallery closed.

In the studio behind the gallery Sian was helping with the upholstering of the six dining chairs, and Langley was concentrating on Deniston Crag. She had plans for Langley's exhibition, and was glad no one had mentioned hers since Sunday. She didn't tell Langley that she was spending more hours than she should each night on that figure, and she didn't really see Barney to tell him. She hardly saw Barney to speak to at all until Wednesday morning, and then as he passed her in the kitchen he said, 'Don't forget to watch television tonight.'

'Natalie,' she said. 'Of course.'

'What about Natalie?' Langley asked. Barney had gone. Now he really was working he was obviously working too hard for anybody supposed to be convalescing, and Emily had been through to old Dr. Murray yesterday suggesting that he came round and had a little chat with Barney.

Dr. Murray had laughed so hard that Emily had held the receiver away from her ear. 'What, me?' he had said. 'I couldn't keep him in bed when he was seven years old. What chance do you think I'll have twenty years later?'

'What about Natalie?' said Langley now, and Emily stopped washing up to hear.

Sian explained, 'She was the girl who phoned that first day.'

'And every other day,' said Emily. 'Unless he phones her.' Emily kept tabs, and she watched Sian when she said it, pleased to see that Sian showed no particular interest.

'And Natalie's an actress,' Sian went on, 'on television tonight. At eight o'clock.'

Langley couldn't see the programme tonight. He had a long-standing invitation to dinner at the home of an expert in antique silver, and it wasn't the sort of home where you could ask them to hush the well-informed conversation and switch on the television. He was sorry about that, he would like to have seen Natalie. 'Although,' as he told Sian, 'so many girls Barney knows are in television or films or the newspapers that you can catch one of them most weeks.'

Well, Emily was going to see Natalie, how about Sian? Sian said she would be watching with Fiona and George. She found she was watching with Barney too when the time came.

Fiona gave the occasion a festive air by producing a dish of savoury rice, and opening a bottle of red wine; and they sat, plates piled high and glasses filled, watching the credit titles slide up the screen.

George informed Barney, 'She always opens a bottle of wine when we watch one of your plays. I don't know if it's supposed to stimulate or deaden the critical faculties.'

'Depends how fast you knock it back,' said Barney.

'Hush,' said Fiona. 'Is that Natalie?'

It was. The very first shot was a close-up of Natalie, and Fiona sighed, 'Life isn't fair, is it?'

Natalie Wender was beautiful: beautiful bones, beautiful skin, and beautiful great swimming eyes looking out of the screen through the veil of hair that was blowing across her face. A man could drown in those eyes, thought Sian. She had read the phrase several times, but she had never seen eyes before that made any sense of it. George said happily, 'Watching her I could feel drunk on a glass of water.'

Sian looked at Barney and he said, 'She can act too.' She could and she did. It was a lightweight play, but quick moving and well produced, and Natalie played her part with more than a little witchery, so that when it ended George and Fiona were in transports over her.

So was Sian. She added her praise to the chorus and Barney said he'd pass it all on, and Natalie would be delighted to hear that they all thought she was terrific.

'Can I give you a hand with these?' said Sian, nodding at the empty plates, and Fiona wrinkled her nose.

'I'll not bother, there's so few, they can go in with the breakfast cups.'

Sian got up. 'Then, if you don't mind, I'll run along. Thank you for the supper and for the show, and Barney, do tell Natalie how much we enjoyed it.'

'I will,' he said.

In her own room Sian looked for a moment at her reflection in the mirror, and wondered how it would feel to look like Natalie. Well, she was never likely to know, and with the memory of Natalie Wender's beauty vivid in her mind her own face looked so plain that she almost threw something at the mirror. Instead she turned her back on it. She had intended to work on her modelling, but decided to write a letter to all at Madame Hélène's, staff and customers, telling them how nicely things were going for her down here. Nothing deeply personal, just a chatty letter that could be handed around, and discussed over the hat selections.

She put it in an envelope and looked around for her purse which had a book of stamps in it. But her purse was in her handbag, and she realized now that she had left that downstairs beside Fiona's settee. She got up to fetch it, and was almost at the top of the stairs when she heard Barney's voice.

She could see him below, his back to her, sitting on the stairs, talking on the telephone. There was nothing to stop her walking down and passing him and going on to knock on the living-room door. Except that he said, 'Missing you? Darling Nattie, you'll never know how much,' so that marching down and pushing by would have been almost as intrusive as though Barney Hollis held Natalie Wender in his arms down there.

Sian backed away, getting into her own room again as quietly as possible. Barney's voice was caressing, lazy and slow and certainly none of her business, and she wasn't listening, but she heard him say, 'And I'll come back with you,' as she closed her door.

So he was going back to London. Fine! thought Sian, he doesn't really fit in here, he's a born disrupter. Fine! so long as Emily and Langley don't worry themselves sick over him.

She wondered where he had phoned Natalie. Most likely at her home, the play had been pre-recorded, she had probably been waiting for him to ring and say what he'd thought about her performance. 'They all thought you were wonderful,' he'd say, and they had and she was. And then she'd asked, 'Are you missing me?' and he'd said, 'Darling Nattie, you'll never know . . .'

He needed Natalie now, he missed her and he needed her, but for how long? A man like Langley would need you always, but a man like Barney didn't really need anybody in the long run. She had never met a case of more innate self-sufficiency. He'd always known where he was going, and he always would. The day when Barney Hollis lost his way would be a long time coming. Still, Natalie was probably equally tough herself. Sian hoped so.

She gave them long enough to finish the phone call, and listened when she opened her door, and hearing no voices went downstairs and looked into the living-room. 'I left my handbag,' she explained. She scooped it from beside the settee, and Fiona said, 'I was telling Barney about the model you're making.'

He was back in the chair from which he had watched the television play. 'I'd like to see it,' he said.

Sian shrugged. 'It's there. Be my guest.'

Barney went with her. He looked at it, and she said, 'I thought it was a woman, but Fiona says it's a rock on a hill she used to know.'

'Is it finished?'

She decided then, 'Yes.' There wasn't anything else to say about it, so she asked, 'How's your play?'

'It's coming.'

'So's Natalie, isn't she?' That rather slipped out. She explained, 'I came out of my room while you were phoning, so I couldn't help overhearing a little.'

'I know,' he said, 'I heard you.'

It was no crime, she hadn't meant to listen. Anyhow he didn't sound as though he suspected her of eavesdropping, and when she asked, 'When's she coming?' he said, 'On Saturday, for the week-end.'

'That will be nice for you both.'

'It will.' He smiled, not at Sian, probably at Natalie. Then he said, 'I'll get this fired for you. There is a kiln behind the gallery, I suppose you know that, but it hasn't been used for some time.'

She said, 'I'd rather not bother Langley with it,' and Barney laughed.

'You're right, it would bother him. It's already bothering Fiona.'

She said, 'Emily's been watching Natalie on the television, she's going to be thrilled when you tell her Natalie's coming for the week-end.'

Emily was more than thrilled, she was slightly horrified. She wasn't used to entertaining such glamorous guests, and the more Barney insisted that Natalie would require nothing that Emily couldn't handle with one arm behind her back the more apprehensive Emily became.

Food now. Emily was sure that Natalie needed a rarefied diet, and fussed about with cookbooks until Langley snapped, 'Emily, the girl's a very minor actress in a very overcrowded profession. She'll probably be glad of a square meal.'

Sian didn't go along with that. She felt sure that Natalie Wender ate regularly and expensively, but it might reassure

Emily if they pretended she didn't.

Sian hadn't mentioned hearing Barney promise to go back with Natalie. It was his place to break that news to his family, not hers, but when Dr. Murray looked in the gallery on Thursday she remembered it.

He rang the street door bell while they were having lunch, and Sian went to see if it was an importunate customer, and brought back the doctor. He was a tall, thin, stooping man, with a deep voice that came surprisingly from his narrow chest. He was also a family friend who had known Barney and Langley all their lives. In theory he was Barney's doctor, although – apart from this little matter of multiple injuries – Barney Hollis hadn't had a day's illness in years.

Dr. Murray had the case history, and had dropped into the stores and climbed up to Nelly's room and told Barney, 'Emily says you're working too hard.'

'Emily,' said Barney, 'fusses too much.'

'She does have that one little weakness,' Dr. Murray allowed, but this time he felt she had cause for concern. He told Barney as much, and now he was telling Emily and Langley. 'He'll do well enough if he doesn't try to be too clever. But he's got to realize he's in worse shape than he's ever been in his life, and he's got to soft pedal a bit. Plenty of sleep, for one thing.'

He chuckled . . . as Barney had said, 'Why not? What's to do here but sleep after ten o'clock? . . .'

Sian asked suddenly, 'You wouldn't say he was fit enough to go back to London yet?' and Dr. Murray looked at her as though she had taken leave of her senses.

'I most certainly would not. There's no question of that, is there?' Without knowing details of the kind of life Barney Hollis habitually led Dr. Murray did know Barney, and felt that no frame that had recently taken that battering should be submitted to that pace.

He looked at Langley rather severely. 'You keep him down here as long as you can. Six months wouldn't be too long.'

'It might be too long for Barney,' said Sian. She was the

one who had asked the question. If Dr. Murray felt like scowling at anyone he should be scowling at her, not at Langley who would have been content to have Barney stay here for ever. She said, 'His girl-friend's coming down this weekend, and what if he wants to go back with her?'

'He'll be a young fool if he does,' said Dr. Murray with decided emphasis.

Langley saw the doctor out and they talked a little longer in the gallery, while in the kitchen Emily confided to Sian that this was one of the penalties of never having had anything wrong with you. When you did come under doctor's orders you couldn't take them seriously.

She didn't resent Barney's robust health, but it had obviously seemed to her a little unfair that Barney should usually miss, and Langley should usually get his share of illness and accident. She had nursed Langley as a child through most of the childish ailments while Barney, if he went down with them at all, always seemed to escape with a minor dose.

Emily loved both brothers, but she felt that life all round bore down harder on Langley. She said, 'You see, in six months' time you won't be able to tell Barney was in that car crash, and poor Langley's got his back for ever.'

Sian bit her lip on a smile. She knew what Emily meant; Langley had had a riding accident as a boy. When he was very overworked and overtired it jabbed still, and gave him the slightest of limps. Sian wouldn't have noticed it if Emily hadn't pointed it out one day. But Emily could be right again, Barney's breaks would probably heal as good as new, and there wouldn't be a jab left between them.

Langley came back and Emily asked, 'Anything else?'

'No, except we've got to watch him.' Langley sat down and smiled wryly. 'And that isn't the easiest thing in the world, is it?'

The arrival of Natalie Wender brightened up Saturday for the whole village. Everyone knew she was coming, and when the red sports car stopped outside the gallery the news went along the high street like jungle drums ... 'Barney

Hollis's girl's arrived, the one who was on the television on Wednesday.' Between Wednesday morning and evening Emily had told enough of her friends to ensure that most T.V. sets in a radius of five miles that night were tuned to Natalie. Now she was here in the flesh, and everyone was anxious for a glimpse of her.

Barney had been waiting for hours, it seemed to Sian. He hadn't gone over to the stores this morning; after breakfast he had come into the studio and lazed around, watching Sian at her upholstering, looking critically at Deniston Crag.

Sian had said, 'It's coming on well,' because Langley wasn't too happy about it. She had been ready to argue every point if Barney said it wasn't, but he didn't. He had just found himself a Victorian pocket set of Chinese checkers and he set them up and began to play with them.

Langley put down his brush and said he thought he'd leave Deniston Crag for today, and Sian didn't blame him. It was having Barney around, even though he was sitting quietly playing Chinese checkers he was still a disturbing influence. You expected him to laugh, or say something. You couldn't work in peace.

Every time the bell rang for a customer or a caller there was a moment of wondering if this was Natalie. Each time Barney bounded up, until Sian said, 'Why don't you open this door, and sit where you can see the other? You're making me drop my tacks, hopping about like a jack-in-the-box.'

Barney grinned at her, 'That's a sound suggestion.' He picked up his checker board and settled himself where he could see straight through into the showroom.

When the red car did arrive Sian was seeing a customer out, and saying her little piece about hoping to see him again. So she saw Natalie get out of the car.

The camera hadn't lied. Natalie Wender was beautiful. Even without the tricks of stage make-up and lighting she was going to be beautiful for the next twenty years at least. She was probably going to be beautiful all her life.

She had come in an open car and her hair was tied back from her face by a wide scarf. Her hair curled around it in small tendrils, and her face gleamed, smooth and almost perfect. She wore a navy blue sleeveless dress, flattish navy blue pumps, and she looked as though she was stepping out of a glossy magazine.

Sian recognized her at once, of course, as the customer went out Natalie came in, and Barney saw her and Natalie saw him and ran to meet him. He put his one good arm around her and said, 'Thank heavens you're here, this has been the longest week of my life.'

'Whose fault's that?' she asked. 'Who made it the longest week?' She stood back a step although he still held her, and looked at him. 'You're feeling better?'

'Now I am.'

'So am I,' she said. 'Much, much better.'

Sian couldn't stand there in the doorway indefinitely, while they beamed at each other. She had to come towards them, towards the studio. 'Ah,' said Barney, 'this is Natalie.'

'Hello,' said Sian.

'And Sian,' said Barney. Natalie smiled at her; she had a lovely dreaming smile. She said, 'Has he been a good patient? Has he done everything the doctor ordered?' She didn't wait for an answer, but turned her smile back on Barney. 'Well now,' she said, 'what now?'

'Come and meet my brother,' said Barney.

Natalie was delighted with Langley. Sian watched her charm spread round and over him, as she almost danced around the studio, loving Deniston Crag, going into raptures at the rocking horse. 'I always wanted one of those,' she said. '*Always*.'

It was quite a little production, with Natalie Wender as the star; and Sian was surprised to find so jaundiced a streak in her own nature, because she had no reason to be jealous. Natalie was charming Langley, as she probably charmed every eligible male, but her sights were firmly set on Barney. He was the one she was watching while she stroked the mane of the rocking horse, and told Langley she thought his painting was super.

When Barney said, 'Now come and say hello to Emily,' she dropped Langley, almost in mid-phrase, and said, 'I'd love to,' and off she went to get Emily under her spell.

My, thought Sian, I'm in a remarkably sour mood this morning! Instead of resenting the girl for looking so gorgeous I should be thanking my stars it's Barney she wants and not Langley.

She said, 'Wow!' and Langley said, 'She seems a nice girl.'

Nice, Sian felt, was an inadequate word to cover Natalie Wender. But she nodded and said, 'Yes.'

Emily's lunch was a great success. They ate in the dining-room today, not the kitchen, and Emily had brought out the silver as though they were entertaining royalty, so that Barney laughed and said, 'Don't think this happens every day,' and Natalie said, 'It looks lovely, all of it, it looks just lovely.'

She had Emily glowing with gratification as she praised each dish and asked for recipes. And I'll bet she can cook too, thought Sian; I'll bet my Victoria sponge wouldn't stand a chance against hers.

Sian had an almost silent meal. There never seemed to be a conversational gap long enough for her to say anything. Barney and Natalie did most of the talking, although Langley joined in occasionally, and Emily sat smiling. Sian smiled, and laughed when the others laughed, but she was glad when the meal ended and she could creep back to the studio. Of course she wasn't jealous, but an hour of sitting opposite Natalie Wender was enough to depress any ordinary run-of-the-mill girl.

When it was opening time for the shop Sian said, 'I'd better get back,' and Langley said, 'I'll be right with you.'

She left them having coffee, and talking about a film in which Natalie had a small part, starting shooting on Tuesday. That was Barney's world. He knew all the names Natalie mentioned. Well, Sian knew most of the names, but

Barney knew them as people, friends. He was important in this world, his status miles higher than Natalie's. They had sent messages and notes. She had a bundle of letters and Barney had said, 'A bit of quiet reading for later.'

Sian opened the shop, and threaded her webbing on yet another dining-room chair. When Langley came she said, 'All go, isn't it?'

'They're welcome to it,' he said.

She sat back on her heels. 'Oh yes,' she said. 'They certainly are.'

When she got back to the stores that night Fiona wanted to know about Natalie, and Sian told her, 'She's just like she looked, she's a knock-out.'

Fiona laughed, 'They have that in common, Barney's girls.'

'Has he brought many down here?'

'He hasn't been down here that much, but he's usually brought somebody with him.'

'Usually girls?'

'Yes,' said Fiona. She was slotting lipsticks into place on a make-up display. She took another from the supply box and slid it into its colour section. She said, 'But the accident's slowed him down for a while I suppose, so Natalie's got that going for her if she really means business.'

'Natalie's got more than that going for her,' said Sian. She watched a customer come up the stairs, with a small boy who darted to the toy shelf, while his mother advanced on the wool section and Fiona turned smiling to help her. 'And I think Natalie does mean business,' said Sian.

Tomorrow Natalie was taking Barney back to London, and tonight Sian was going to the cinema with Langley. She made up and dressed with care, and would have been fairly satisfied with herself if she hadn't kept seeing Natalie Wender at every turn. Not literally. Sian was in her bedsitter and Natalie was somewhere or other with Barney. But when you had really worked on the overall effect it was disheartening to know that if Natalie Wender fell head first into a ditch and crawled out again she would still look more glamorous than you did now.

The film wasn't much help either. Everybody in it seemed miserable from beginning to end, and Langley was in a thoughtful mood.

Over supper in her room afterwards Sian tried very hard to be half as gay and entertaining as Natalie and knew she was missing by a mile. She had left a chicken casserole in Fiona's oven and that was good and they ate it, but the evening had lacked sparkle. Natalie and Barney hadn't gone out; they were having a quiet evening at home, Langley had told her, and Sian wondered whether Langley, sitting here with her, was thinking that once again Barney was the lucky one: Barney with Natalie, Langley with Sian.

When Langley looked broodingly into his coffee cup she did ask, 'Is anything the matter?' and he said,

'Of course not.' Then he added, 'You don't think Barney is considering going back, do you?'

While she tried to decide how to answer that Langley went on, 'Because you mentioned it to Dr. Murray, and Natalie seems to think he is. She's talking about next week as though she and Barney are going to be together.'

Sian said, 'What does Barney say? Why don't you ask him?' That was so obvious an answer that she was bewildered, and Langley made a little gesture almost of apology.

'I know it sounds ridiculous, but if I start arguing about it that's the certain way to get him to pack up and go. Try fencing him in and he's got to get out. I suppose he still sees me as the older brother who used to lay down the law once upon a time.'

She said, 'I never heard anything so stupid,' and Langley sighed, 'It is, isn't it? Ah well, I suppose all we can do is hope for the best, because he's certainly not fit enough to leave. It must sound very stupid to you.'

'It does,' she said emphatically, then she relented and smiled, 'Don't worry, Natalie Wender's so wonderful she's bound to be a born nurse. With her hovering round with nourishing soup he should make the get-well record.'

But Langley wasn't amused. He sighed again. This time Sian sighed with him and said wearily, 'Then all I can suggest is knock-out drops in his coffee, and lock him in the cellars till she's gone.'

Langley didn't appreciate that solution either. Shortly afterwards he kissed her good night, and that was that. She closed the side door of the stores after him, and climbed the stairs slowly back to her own room, reflecting that she had a headache and that it had been a distinctly unrewarding day ...

This Sunday morning Sian helped Fiona with the cooking, and then they both helped George with the floor polishing. She had her meal with Fiona and George and afterwards went over to the gallery. She had promised last night; she had declined an invitation to dinner, but she said that of course she would look in to say good-bye to Natalie, and possibly to Barney.

She let herself into the gallery, and went through the door at the far end that led into the house. That opened into a square hall containing the stairs and more doors. The door to the kitchen was open, and Emily came out as though she had been waiting for Sian. She said, 'He's going back.'

'Is he?' said Sian.

Emily was pink-faced and flustered. 'You know what the doctor said. He's not fit. Langley's round there now, gone to see if Dr. Murray will come and have a word with him.'

'I thought Dr. Murray had had his word,' said Sian, 'and a lot of listening Barney seems to have done. Where are they?'

Emily indicated the door to the drawing-room. 'She's in there, he's packing.'

'Right,' said Sian. 'Not that he'll listen to me, but I might as well have my say.'

She ran upstairs and rapped on the door of the bedroom she knew as Barney's. He called, 'Come in.' He had a half-packed case on the bed, and was sitting looking at it as though he was checking contents. When he saw Sian he said, 'Hello.'

84

She said, 'You can't go, you know.'

'What?' He'd heard her first time. He said 'Why?' before she had time to repeat it, and she said, 'Oh, don't be so pig-headed, you know what the doctors said. I know you're bored down here, we're a very boring lot, and where Natalie comes from everybody's bright and beautiful, but surely you can stick it a little longer. If your work means anything to you you'll have to stick it won't you, because that's what they told you, wasn't it, you couldn't work and racket around?'

Barney said, 'Mind your own business, love, you're not one of the family yet.'

She said bitterly, 'You just don't care that you're leaving Emily bothered sick, and Langley worried sleepless about you!'

'One of my earliest memories,' said Barney, 'is Langley worried sleepless about me.'

She flounced the length of the room and back again, too irritated to stand still. 'I don't understand any of them. Why they want you here or she wants you there, or anybody wants you anywhere. Nor can I understand why you haven't enough sense to remember you didn't come out of that car your old sweet self. You came out of it half dead, and as Dr. Murray says you're still in worse shape than you've ever been in your life.'

'I know it,' said Barney. He still sat on the bed, and his eyes in the scarred face were bleak. She had never seen them bleak before, and they silenced her, checking the flood of hot words.

He said with distant irony, 'You could have spared the histrionics. I stopped fooling myself I could go back yet half an hour ago.'

'Oh!' She said nothing more and neither did he. Then he got up and took a tie out of the case and she asked, with some idea of conciliation, 'May I unpack for you?'

'I do have strength enough for that.' He opened a drawer and tosssed in the tie. His voice was harsh and impatient as though he hated the weakness that chained him here. She felt that he was a hairsbreadth from smashing his good fist against the walls and she tried facile comfort,

'It won't be for long. Only a month or so.'

He said savagely, 'For God's sake stop humouring me!'

'Then stop—' He rode roughshod over whatever it was she was trying to say. He said, 'You've seen Natalie. Surely even you can realize that if I'm away from a girl like that for long I'm going to lose her.'

CHAPTER FIVE

SHE had been quite unforgivably clumsy. She had known he wanted to go back with Natalie, but she hadn't realized it was because he was afraid of losing her. From what she had seen with her own eyes she would have thought it was the other way round, but apparently she was wrong. Things, as they say, are rarely as they seem, and Sian had her first pang of pity for Barney Hollis.

All the same she found herself asking, 'If you can't trust her unless you're watching her, what kind of loving is that?' It sounded priggish, and he began to smile.

'Let's say temptation's easier to come by in the big city.'

'So?'

'So don't be too sanctimonious. How do you know how you'd stand up to it? Can you cross your heart you'd come through unscathed?'

He caught her arm, just above the elbow, and held her, smiling down at her. There was no bleakness in his eyes now or anger in his voice, just the old gleam of mockery, as though he regretted having dropped his guard by admitting how he felt about Natalie, and was wiping it out by teasing Sian.

He was attractive, and he knew it. He could be overwhelmingly attractive and Sian stiffened, suddenly terrified that if he drew her close and kissed her hard she might go up like bracken in high summer.

She wrenched herself free and made her voice as mocking as his. 'Don't practise your wiles on me, and don't tell me you'll be eating your heart out for Natalie or anybody else. How long do your grand passions usually last?'

She hoped this grand passion wasn't real, because it would be hellish to care deeply for someone and not trust them at all. But maybe he was wrong. Natalie Wender might be an actress, but she had shown every sign of being mightily struck with Barney Hollis.

'Sian Rowan,' he said, 'you're a cynical wench.'

'Cynical and sanctimonious,' she intoned solemnly, 'that about covers it. Now I'll go and break the news to the family that they're stuck with you for a while longer.'

Langley hadn't come back yet. Emily was still in the kitchen, cutting sandwiches into tiny little triangles and building a pyramid with them. Sian said, 'It's all right, he isn't going.'

Emily had to sit down to recover. 'It's such a relief,' she kept saying, 'such a relief.' And then, 'How did you manage it?'

Sian disclaimed credit. 'Nothing to do with me, he'd decided before I started talking.'

Emily babbled on, while Sian took over the cutting of the sandwiches. Whether he cared or not Barney Hollis was a major part of Emily's life. Langley had been the blessing and the comfort, Barney the maverick, the one who brought the heartaches.

While Sian finished the top of the pyramid, placing a final sandwich on the very apex, Emily did a run through of life with the Hollis boys, ending as Sian turned from the table, 'Well, it could be a blessing in disguise, that car crash. He'd have forgotten he'd got a brother unless something like this had happened.'

'Let's hope he remembers in future,' said Sian, and Emily nodded in fervent assent.

'Where do you want the sandwiches?' Sian asked.

'In the drawing-room,' said Emily. 'I thought I'd give them a bite to eat and a cup of tea before they went.'

The drawing-room door was open and as Sian crossed the hall from the kitchen she heard Natalie. Barney had broken the news, it seemed, and Natalie was saying in the tones of one looking on the bright side, 'At least I won't have to worry what you're getting up to down here. I haven't seen any girl around you're likely to look twice at.'

Her lovely clear actress's voice rang out, so that when Sian arrived in the doorway it was obvious that Sian had heard what she said. Natalie gasped, and made a comical grimace, and Sian laughed. She didn't want them to think she was embarrassed. She put down the sandwiches on a little round table and said, 'But you haven't seen Nelly. Nell is Barney's secret passion.'

She said it as a joke, but Natalie's face hardened, and she turned narrowed eyes on Barney. 'Who's Nell?'

'The local legend,' he said. 'Nell Gwynn slept here.'

'*Here?*'

'In the village. Over the road.'

She gurgled with laughter. 'You're nuts,' she said, and reached up to ruffle his hair, and he took her hand and held it, and Sian said, 'I'll get the tea.'

Langley arrived as they were pouring water into the teapot. Dr. Murray had been out on a case, and Langley had waited, but he hadn't come back. When Emily said, 'He's changed his mind anyway,' Langley looked as relieved as she had been when Sian had told her.

So then Emily took tea for Barney and Natalie into the drawing-room, and Sian and Langley and Emily had theirs in the kitchen. That seemed tactful and kindly, because if Natalie wanted to reach home before dark she mustn't leave it much later.

They all waved good-bye, standing on the pavement in front of the gallery. It was a gay little send-off, with Natalie thanking Emily, and telling Langley and Sian it had been lovely meeting them, and looking at Barney with luminous eyes that said far more than her lips were saying.

The red car gathered speed and Barney went back into the gallery and into the house. Emily followed. Sian and Langley paused for a moment in the gallery when Langley said, 'Thank you for persuading him to stay.'

'But I didn't. Like I told you, he'd realized he'd do better to stay.'

Langley still looked at her gratefully. 'Barney doesn't have so much. No real home, no roots.'

She said, 'He's got Natalie. She seems a pretty good consolation prize.'

89

Langley smiled and shook his head. 'There are so many things more important than mere physical beauty.' He must have realized as he said it that it wasn't the happiest of compliments, because he went on quickly, 'And you're beautiful too.'

'Oh, I am,' she said gaily. 'I'm always stopping the traffic in the high street.'

She felt ridiculously light-hearted, and when Langley looked surprised she said contritely, 'I'm sorry; I'm not laughing at you. I know I'm not as beautiful as the Natalie Wenders of the world. Of course I do, and of course it doesn't matter.'

Well, not too much! It would be nice to look like Natalie, but then it would be nice to have wings. One managed without.

'Let's go somewhere,' she said. She felt that Barney would rather be alone for a while, or at least not have any more folk around than was absolutely necessary.

'Of course, where would you like to go?'

'Deniston Crag?' She hadn't seen it, but she knew it wasn't too far away, and it was early evening and summer.

She recognized it from Langley's painting before he said, 'There you are.' It was a local beauty spot on the bend of a river, the crag overhung the green sward and there had been picnickers who had left litter around. But it was still pretty. They parked the car and walked down to the river. The sun was setting in a haze of soft pinks and blues, and it was peaceful, hardly a ripple on the river.

Afterwards they had a drink at a local pub, and talked about an auction tomorrow and what Langley should bid for. Then they drove back. She didn't say, 'Come in,' it was late and she was tired, and when Langley asked, 'Will you come back for coffee?' she said, 'No, thanks, but thank you for the evening and I'll see you in the morning.'

'Yes indeed,' he said.

As she reached her landing she saw the faint strip of light round the not-too-well-fitting door of the storeroom. She hadn't noticed it from the street, but she hadn't consciously looked up, and the diamond-paned window was set so that the moonlight silvered it.

George and Fiona weren't usually to be found in their storeroom this late on a Sunday night, so it had to be Barney. She opened the door, and he sat in the window alcove with a lamp on the table. 'Working?' she asked.

'What do you think I'm doing, conducting a seance?'

In the pool of lamplight with the shadows around he could have been. She came in, closing the door, and made for the archway to her own room. She said, 'If you get Nell call me. I'd like a chat with her.'

'If I get Nell,' he said, 'I'm calling nobody.'

She laughed, swishing aside the curtain and stepping through, and when he asked, 'Do you mind if I'm here a little longer?' she said, 'Why should I? You're fully occupied, aren't you?'

She was glad he was working. It meant that he wasn't sitting brooding about Natalie, and if he worked himself into exhaustion he'd sleep when he got home. Work for Barney was therapy right now.

She kicked off her shoes and sat on the divan, her feet tucked under her, her cheek resting on the cushioned back, listening to the typewriter tapping. She thought drowsily for a while about tomorrow, the things she had to do. She thought about Deniston Crag, and the fluffy clouds round the sunset, and from there she drifted into sleep.

She woke and she was stiff, and knew she must have been sleeping for an hour or so. As she stretched she heard the typewriter again and looked at her watch and saw it was after midnight. If he chose to work all night that was his look-out, but she'd offer to get him a drink before she turned in herself.

She crossed to the archway and pulled the curtain aside and went into the storeroom. Barefoot she made little noise, and he was engrossed in what he was doing so that he didn't notice her until she stood in the lamplight, then he looked up and smiled. 'Hello, Nell,' he said.

'Sorry,' she said, 'wrong wavelength. Are you staying the night?'

'Is that an offer?'

'It is not, as well you know. But if you are working on can I get you some coffee or something?'

He looked at his wristwatch and whistled. 'Thanks, I'll be on my way.'

'You needn't on my account, the typewriter doesn't bother me, but Dr. Murray did say early nights and this is verging on a late one.'

'You're right,' he said. He got up, said, 'Good night,' and pressed the button on the lamp so that the only light came through Sian's linen curtain. It was enough to see your way between the packing cases, and Barney reached the door without bumping into anything. In the open doorway he turned, 'Good night, Nell,' he said.

'Good night,' said Sian, in a husky and seductive voice from the shadows . . .

'Good morning,' said Langley, with a hint of chill, next morning as she walked into the kitchen of the Little Gallery with the mail. Barney wasn't around, Emily was. Everything seemed as usual and Sian looked hard at Langley, wondering if she imagined the edginess.

She was here at her customary time, but he had finished his breakfast, and he finished his coffee as she watched him, picked up the mail and said, 'I'll be in the studio, I have some phoning to do.'

'All right.' She sat where she usually sat and waited till the door closed, then she asked Emily, 'Is anything the matter with Langley? Has anything happened?'

Emily tutted, 'Don't ask me.'

'But I am asking you. What's going on?'

'I don't know,' said Emily doggedly.

Sian poured herself a cup of coffee and buttered a piece of toast and took them with her into the studio. Langley was opening the mail, sitting in front of the typewriter, and Sian put down her plate and said, 'I can't be imagining double, not you and Emily *both* out of sorts. What's the matter?'

He was just tearing an envelope. He took out the letter and frowned at it, then looked up at Sian, and said abruptly, 'Will you marry me?'

She didn't know what she had expected, but she hadn't expected this. She almost dropped the coffee cup she was still holding, then she said, 'Why am I getting a proposal now?' because it needed explaining.

Langley got up. He looked wretched. He said, 'It's wrong, isn't it? The timing, everything. Why didn't I ask you yesterday at Deniston Crag?'

That would have been a more romantic setting. Not that there was anything jarring about the studio, Sian was very fond of it, but as a proposal of marriage this was puzzling. She said, 'I don't know. Why didn't you? And why the rush now? What happened between last night and this morning?'

Langley said, 'I'm a fool, I shouldn't have done it like this. I didn't mean to. I meant to ask you to marry me, but not to blurt it out like that.'

She said again, 'What happened between last night and this morning?'

Langley said, 'Barney—'

'Yes?' Her voice was quiet. She would have thought that Barney Hollis had enough troubles going in his own right, and he had promised to keep out of this particular problem. If he had had a man-to-man talk with Langley and informed him that Sian was eating her heart out with love for Langley she would, so help her, murder him! She said, 'What did Barney say to you?'

Langley said, 'He didn't come back until well after midnight. I thought he was in. When he came in I asked him where he'd been and he said working, over at the stores.'

'That's where he was.'

'He was there when you went up to your room, after we said good night?'

'Yes.'

'Waiting for you?'

She began to laugh, then changed her mind. 'No.'

'But you did talk to him?'

'We must have exchanged all of half a dozen phrases.'

'But he was there, and he stayed there.'

'Not in my room.'

'In a connecting room, with not even a door between.'

She supposed it was flattering. It certainly proved Barney's point that a little jealousy might wake Langley up. She supposed she should be grateful that Barney hadn't gone on working all night, while she slept calm and untroubled on her own side of the curtain. If Langley was this concerned by Barney returning at midnight goodness knows what he'd have made of him coming home at dawn.

And it was so crazy. She could feel laughter twitching her lips, and knew if she smiled she would begin to giggle and she had small hopes of Langley seeing the joke.

She said, 'Remember Natalie? Barney's very fond of her, I think he's in love with her.'

Langley said, 'Barney's in love with nobody. He never has been and he never will be. He doesn't know what love means.'

She had never heard Langley speak so bitterly. He looked tired, almost old, and she said gently, 'Maybe he doesn't show it, but I'm sure he loves you and Emily.'

'In his way,' said Langley.

She couldn't argue with that. Langley went on, 'Barney's always been able to make people like him, without trying and without caring. He's my brother, I'd do anything in the world for him, but I know how callous he can be.'

She had no doubt that Langley did know. He went to the window and stood, his shoulders hunched a little, looking out across the large flagstoned yard to the outbuildings. There wasn't much to see. He said, 'Last night I asked him to keep away from you and he laughed.'

She had nearly laughed herself. But she was sure Langley had passed a grim night, and that he needed reassurance so badly that Barney might have given him a little instead of laughing at him. She said, 'Because it was nonsense, because

94

he thought you must be joking.'

Langley said, 'When you're wearing my ring he'll know it isn't a joke. I think then—'

She said, 'So that's why you're asking me to marry you in such a hurry – to save me from Barney?'

'*No!*' He spun round from the window. 'I'm asking you to marry me because I love you, I want you for my wife. I want you here always, with me.'

He was utterly sincere. Of course he was asking her to marry him because he loved her, but the reason he was asking her at this particular moment was to keep her safe from Barney, and that was too much chivalry. She looked at him and felt tenderness course through her, and almost took him in her arms. He needed comforting, he was so sensitive, so vulnerable.

The bell rang on the street door. Not the bell that warned that someone was coming in, the press button bell outside, because the shop wasn't open although it was ten past nine.

'Damn them,' said Langley furiously. 'Sian, will you marry me?'

She said, 'Next time you ask me, perhaps.'

'How long do you need to think about it?'

It wasn't so much time as a different set of circumstances. She didn't feel she was being unreasonable in wanting the moment when Langley asked her to marry him to be theirs alone, and not because Langley had had a row with Barney the night before.

She smiled and put a hand on Langley's arm. 'We'll go to Deniston Crag again.' That was a promise, and he said, 'Bless you,' and she said, 'I'll see who's anxious to get in. We don't usually have customers so eager.'

As she hurried down the gallery towards the street door she wondered – why didn't I say yes, and never mind that he'd been stampeded into asking me? Barney would tell her she was a fool, so would Fiona, so would anyone she confided in, so she'd better tell none of them. And that was a lovely secret. Langley had asked her to marry him, and he would again very soon, and then she would say yes, and then they'd tell the whole world.

She opened the door and the girl on the step said, 'Eggs, duck eggs. Emily wanted some.'

She had a small basketful of duck eggs, and a shooting brake parked at the kerbside. She was a plump and pretty girl, with the endearing anxious-to-please air of a puppy. 'Hello,' said Sian. 'I'm sorry the door was still locked, do come in.'

Phyllis Barker came in. She bought most of her clothes from Fiona, and Sian had met her in the stores several times. There was an inevitable wariness between the two girls because Phyllis had once had a schoolgirl crush on Langley, and three years and four boy-friends later, still envied anyone who had the joy of working with him.

When Langley had advertised for an assistant in the gallery Phyllis had done a little dreaming, but shorthand and typing were stipulated and all she was trained for was helping her mother run the farmhouse. And she knew that if she did apply half the village would start laughing at her again, and her boy-friend and her parents would be furious with her, and she probably wouldn't get the job anyway. She thought Sian was very lucky and life wasn't fair.

She chattered as they walked through the gallery about the weather and the size of the duck eggs, and when Langley came to the studio door, her already light voice went even higher. 'Why, hello,' she said, as though he was the last person she would have expected to meet in his own shop. She held out the basket of duck eggs and explained, 'Emily was asking my mother about them.'

Emily and Mrs. Barker were both W.I. members, Mrs. Barker had brought along an oven-ready duck to be raffled, proceeds towards the Old Folks' Fund, and Emily had said that duck eggs made a nice rich cake but you couldn't get them too often these days. So Phyllis had brought her some duck eggs.

Now Langley smiled and thanked her, and her cheeks went pink. Sian said laconically, 'You'll find Emily through there. You know the way?'

'Oh *yes*,' said Phyllis. 'Yes, I do.'

Langley opened the door into the hall for her and she smiled tremulously up at him. Sian smiled too, and as soon as the door was closed and Phyllis and her duck eggs on their way to Emily, she said, 'Now if *I* had a jealous nature—'

'What?' said Langley. 'That child?'

'That is no child,' protested Sian. 'In years or anything else.' She was fooling, and Langley laughed. He went back into the studio to collect his briefcase. He said, 'There's nothing in the mail you can't handle. I'll get away as soon as I can.' The auction would last the day, but the items he intended to bid for would probably come up before lunch.

'Get some bargains,' said Sian.

'I hope I have,' said Langley. 'I hope I've got the best bargain of all.' He could hardly kiss her, especially as someone was looking in the window. He squeezed her hand instead, and she said, 'Good luck.'

The mail was straightforward. He had opened it all, but he hadn't done anything about it, at the time his mind had been on other things, and now Sian sat down in front of the typewriter and answered the letters that needed quick replies, made notes where notes were needed, and filed a list and a couple of catalogues.

Phyllis, on her way out, opened the studio door and looked in, her disappointment at finding no Langley so undisguised that Sian said, 'Sorry, he's gone to an auction.'

'Langley?' said Phyllis, colouring brightly. She came in and looked around her. She saw Deniston Crag and stood in front of it, then she said, 'That's marvellous, isn't it?'

'I think it's good.'

'Oh, I think it's marvellous.' She turned back to Sian. 'Do you like working here?'

'Very much.'

Phyllis sighed deeply. Yesterday she had had a row with her boy-friend, and when her mother had said over breakfast this morning, 'I must remember to send Emily Parkinson a few duck eggs,' Phyllis had offered, 'I'll take them. I've got to go down to the village.'

Her mother had hesitated. Memories of Phyllis mooning over Langley Hollis came back to her. They didn't want any of that again. After last night's break with Gordon, Phyllis was depressed enough without raking up past heartaches. Not very lucky in love, Phyllis was turning out to be. Mrs. Barker had said, 'There's no hurry,' and Phyllis had said, 'I'll take them now.'

Now Sian looked up and saw with horror that Phyllis's eyes were swimming with tears. One tear brimmed over and slipped, plump and perfect, down her cheek, and Sian jumped to her feet and said, 'Come and sit down, whatever it is can't be that bad.'

'I know,' said Phyllis. She hated the tears. She hated the way she blushed, the way she couldn't hide anything she was feeling. She looked at this girl who was cool and composed, and who they said Langley was falling for and Barney had taken out, and shame that Sian should see her weep made the tears scald her eyes. She shut her eyes tight, squeezing the tears through wet lashes, and unable, blinded, to find her handkerchief, so that she had to rub them away with the back of her hand. Sian led her to a chair, and put a tissue in her fingers, and Phyllis finished dabbing the dampness with the tissue and announced, hiccupping, that life was horrible.

'It can be,' Sian agreed.

'I had a row with Gordon yesterday,' said Phyllis. Gordon Wilkes, Sian remembered Emily and Fiona telling her, was supposed to be marrying Phyllis in the spring. She said, 'Oh, Phyllis, I'm sorry.'

Phyllis hiccupped again. 'It wouldn't have worked anyway, but it still makes you feel awful, doesn't it?'

Sian was sure it did. There was a bottle of brandy in the cupboard. She poured a generous measure, and handed it to Phyllis, who goggled at it. 'I'm driving,' said Phyllis.

'Drink it,' Sian advised, 'and walk.'

Phyllis giggled, and looked surprised at herself. 'Go on,'

Sian urged, and Phyllis raised the glass with desperate resolution and took a good deep gulp. Then she waited for
about five seconds, and announced that she felt better.

'Good,' said Sian. She sat on one of the newly up-
holstered dining chairs and said, 'I'd better not join you, the
customers might notice. But you drink that, and then we'll
have some coffee.'

'Thank you,' said Phyllis.

'It's nice to have a visitor,' said Sian.

'I shouldn't have come here this morning,' Phyllis admitted, 'but I felt so miserable, and Langley's so kind, isn't
he?'

What kind of kindness did Phyllis have in mind? Sian
wondered. Phyllis said, 'I just felt I'd like to talk to him. I
used to have quite a crush on him – oh, years ago. I made
rather an idiot of myself, and of course he wasn't interested
in me except as a friend, but he always seemed to understand, you could always talk to him.'

'He'll be back this afternoon.'

Phyllis sipped a little more brandy. She said, 'It wasn't a
very good idea, making a nuisance of myself.'

Sian couldn't really see what Langley was expected to do.
As Phyllis had decided that marriage with Gordon wouldn't
have worked she obviously didn't want advice on how to
patch up a quarrel. And if she had come along hoping that
Langley, always so kind and understanding, might offer
more than friendship this time, perhaps the best thing would
be to say, 'He asked me to marry him less than half an hour
ago.' Except that that might throw Phyllis into a state that
would need the rest of the brandy and an ambulance.

When the doorbell rang Sian said, 'I'll be right back,' and
came out to attend to her customer. It wasn't a customer, it
was Barney, and she looked at him without affection. 'I
want to talk to you.'

'What about?'

She looked over her shoulder, towards the door of the
studio. 'Wait, though, I've got Phyllis Barker in there.
She's had a quarrel with her boy-friend and she wanted to

tell Langley about it.' Barney grinned, and Sian said sharply, 'And it isn't funny.'

'Oh, I don't know,' said Barney.

'Well, I do, and Langley's away till this afternooon, so what do we do with Phyllis?'

'If that's her car outside we could send her home.'

'No, we can't just yet. I've just given her a brandy.'

Barney shook his head. 'You do like to complicate things, don't you?'

She said crossly, 'She was upset, she needed a drink, and talking about complications, will you *please* stop pretending to Langley that you've got designs on me. He was really worried about last night.'

'He was, wasn't he?' said Barney happily. 'I think it was the after-midnight touch that got him. Midnight seems to have a sort of mystique about it. Somehow the idea of you and me both being under George McDade's eaves after twelve o'clock has a strange significance for Langley. Anyhow,' he grinned at her, 'it's working, isn't it? He's getting more proprietorial by the minute.'

... Possessive enough to say, 'I want you for my wife, I want you here with me always.' But that was none of Barney's business yet ...

She said firmly, 'Just stop it now, will you? I don't want to play puppet-on-a-string any more.' She added for good measure, 'If you really believe you can fix real life as easily as the things you write about, fix it for yourself and Natalie.'

It was a legitimate parry, but for a moment he winced as though pain caught him. Then he laughed, 'Ah, but it's harder to pull the strings by remote control.'

She said, 'For what it's worth I don't think you'll lose her. I think when you whistle Natalie will come running.'

Phyllis came out of the studio, and Barney raised his good hand in greeting. 'Hello, Phyllis.' She came towards them slowly. 'You're looking more delectable every time I see you,' said Barney.

'Am I?' She smiled wistfully. 'Oh, I wish I was!' She

included Sian in her smile. 'You know, I think I am going to walk home. It's only ten minutes or so, but I think I'd better. I'll send somebody to fetch the car.'

'All right,' said Sian.

Phyllis went carefully, negotiating bric-à-brac with a measuring eye. In the street she waved at them through the window and Barney asked, 'How much brandy did you give her?'

'A double, I suppose, and it was Langley's best. The one he clinches super deals with. Anyhow, she brought Emily some duck eggs.'

'I hope Langley considers duck eggs a fair deal for his vintage hooch,' said Barney. 'By the way I came to tell you you've had an offer for your woman who looks like a rock.'

'What? Somebody wants to *buy* the thing?'

'That's what Joss has just told me.'

'Who's Joss?'

'Joss Ennerman. He's coming over to talk to you tonight. He's got a gallery and he exhibits for some of the biggest living names. He's had an offer for your woman, and it isn't even fired yet, it's still drying out.'

That was exciting. She asked 'How much?' and when he told her, '*No*! You don't mean it?'

'He quite fancies the head too, but that's mine and I've got your deed of gift.'

'Oh, my stars! I've never sold anything in my life before. Except the miniatures, of course.'

It was a fluke, but it was rather gorgeous. She said, 'What *will* Langley say?' savouring in anticipation his surprise and pleasure, and Barney said, 'Don't bank on too many congratulations.'

'What do you mean?'

Barney shrugged. 'It's not Langley's kind of art. He may feel you're being overpaid.'

'He may be right. But it isn't likely to happen again, is it, so let me enjoy it.'

A middle-aged man and woman peering in the window looked as though they might be her first customers of the day. She watched them hopefully, and smiled as they opened the door. 'That's right, love,' said Barney, 'you enjoy it.'

It was a sale. Not a large one, but the Little Gallery survived on little sales, and Sian wrapped up the framed cross-stitch sampler reading 'Home is Where the Heart is', and agreed that it would be a very suitable present to take to a housewarming.

As the couple got back into their car, parked just behind Phyllis's shooting brake, Barney said, 'They're going to hang that little gem on somebody's wall?'

'And why not? I know it's trite and maudlin, but I think it's rather sweet.'

'That was the Victorians,' said Barney, 'all heart.'

'I'll look out for a sampler for you – anywhere I hang my hat is home.'

'I don't wear a hat,' said Barney.

She wished Langley would phone. She wanted to tell him about selling the model, because she knew he'd be pleased. And tonight, after she'd seen this Joss Ennerman, perhaps she and Langley could celebrate somewhere. He might ask her to marry him again and she would say yes.

In the meantime, in celebration mood, she could paint a few more spots on the rocking horse. She began to open the tin of pink paint and Barney said, 'Oh, and before I forget, don't sell it.'

The lid lifted and she took it off gingerly, placing it on a piece of typing paper. He was talking about the horse, and she knew before he said, 'I want it for Natalie.'

She said, 'Sorry, it's sold.'

'Who bought it?' He was going to phone and tell them the whole thing was a mistake, the assistant had not realized the rocking horse was sold already. Our deepest apologies, and do come in and choose a small thing on the house to show how sorry we are you have been inconvenienced. Like Langley said, Barney took it for granted that anything he wanted he could get, and he wanted the rocking horse for Natalie.

Sian said, 'I have.' She wanted it too, she had done all along, and now with this unexpected windfall to add to her microscopic savings she could afford it. She pleaded, 'Please get Natalie something else.'

She went round to the head of the wooden horse, and touched the wide eyes and the flaring nostrils. The man who had carved this head had made it proud and beautiful, and Sian stroked it with gentle covetous fingers. 'I've been putting off finishing him because I knew he'd be sold as soon as Langley put him on show, and now I've got a little money I can buy him. He'd only be a gimmick for Natalie, wouldn't he? But he's an old friend to me.'

After childhood rocking horses were gimmicks, but this in her bed-sitter would be like an old friend. She twined her fingers in the nylon silk of the long brown mane, as though she expected Barney to grab the horse there and then and ship it off without further ado.

He said, 'Relax. He's yours. Stop glaring. I've no doubt we can find Natalie another.'

'Yes, of course you can, Langley will find one for you.' She was quite absurdly elated, and anxious to get away with her prize before he had time to change his mind. She said, 'As soon as Langley comes we'll take him over, I'll finish his spots at home.'

She knew just where she would put him; he would do wonders for the decor of her bed-sitter, he'd lift it right out of the painted-tin-trays class. She said gaily, 'He'll be someone to talk to, after midnight.'

Barney stroked the smooth painted neck where the toy maker had carved rippling muscles. He said, 'After midnight he might sprout wings. You might ride over the house-tops.'

'Shall we bring you back a star?'

'It would seem the least you could do.' He patted the horse. 'I'll tell George to expect a horse round.'

Her delight lasted, blissfully including customers and phone calls for the rest of the morning. There were two more customers and three phone calls and she dealt with them all tenderly. She was happy. Langley had told her he loved her, and asked her to marry him. And, although it was a tiny thing by comparison with that, buying the rocking horse was the biggest treat she had ever had in her life. She had never had any money for extravagant gestures, and she wasn't the kind of girl, like Natalie Wender, who gets rocking horses or orchids or emerald rings bought for her.

She waited for Langley to come back, and when he did she ran to meet him. It was as near lunch time as made no matter; she slipped the lock on the door as he came in and asked, 'How did it go?'

He sounded less exuberant than she felt. 'Oh, not too good. The prices went too high.'

'Did you get anything?'

'Some china, nothing that's going to make our fortunes. It was all rather a waste of time.'

She slipped her hand through his arm. 'Talking of fortunes, I might be able to help you.' She laughed. 'The silliest thing happened to me. You remember that head I modelled?'

He had to think to remember, then he said, 'Yes?'

'Well, I made something else, a model of a woman, and Barney said he'd get it fired for me, and it seems a friend of his took it, a Joss Ennerman.'

Langley's mouth turned down slightly. She said, 'And somebody's bought it.' She told him how much, and he said, 'That's good, that's very good.'

'It's crazy.'

'You didn't tell me you were doing another model.'

'Well, it didn't seem important. I just—'

'But you showed it to Barney.'

'Well, he was there. He—' It was being spoiled. She had wanted Langley to laugh about it with her, but instead he was back on this stupid groundless jealousy of Barney. She had explained, she had *told* him.

He said impatiently, 'All right, Barney sold it for you. That's fine, that's marvellous, but don't think this means you can rely on him to go on helping if you're considering modelling as a commercial proposition.'

She hadn't expected anything of the sort. She said sharply, 'I won't, but this was kind of him. It was a little trouble to take and I'm grateful.'

'Of course you are,' said Langley. 'Why not? If Barney's got Joss Ennerman to handle your stuff you're half way there.'

They were at the door leading from the gallery into the house. He stood for a moment, then seemed to change his mind, and instead of opening that door strode into the studio.

Sian was half prepared to leave him to it. He wasn't pleased at her news, but what did he want her to do, for goodness' sake? Refuse to take the money? Promise not to make any more models without Langley's seal of approval?

Because she had been so thrilled his reaction was the more depressing. It had taken all the gaiety away. When Langley called her name from the studio she still hesitated, standing in the gallery. She wasn't going to be scolded as though she and Barney had been in cahoots on a secret project, deliberately excluding Langley. Langley had it all out of proportion.

But she went. Langley said, as she came into the room, 'I'm sorry. Of course it's good news, it's very good news. But I've just had a disappointing morning, and when you told me,' he smiled with bitter nostalgia, 'it sounded like the old tale all over again. Everything Barney touches goes easily. You make a model; Barney sells it for you without any trouble, for a damn sight more than I could have got if I'd put it on show here.'

She went with quick sympathy towards him. 'What does it matter who sold it?'

'I'll tell you something.' Langley put an arm around her, and held her close. 'It's something I try to forget, but I want to tell you.'

She stood very still. She didn't even raise her head so that she could see his face. He said huskily, 'My father had been ailing for some time before he died, but when the end came there was warning of it. Not much, Dr. Murray gave him a matter of hours. Nothing could be done. He was rushed into hospital, but we knew it was the end.

'I rang Barney. I told Barney he was dying. It was a Saturday night, early. He lived till Sunday morning and each time he became conscious he called for Barney. He never stopped calling for Barney.

'Barney arrived a couple of hours too late. He could have got here nine hours before, but he left it till morning; he thought even death would wait for him.'

That night Langley must have come close to hating his brother. It wasn't hate now, but it still smouldered, it was still remembered.

Sian ventured. 'Perhaps he didn't realize how ill—'

'He knew,' said Langley shortly. 'I told him.' He put a hand in front of his eyes. 'I'm only telling you now because you mustn't rely on Barney for anything. He's generous enough, so long as no one's making real demands. Beyond that, the answer is no.'

'I'll remember,' she said.

She thought there could surely be no more dreadful death than to die calling for someone you loved who never came.

CHAPTER SIX

EMILY took a quick look at Langley as he and Sian came into the kitchen, and was relieved to see that little mis-understanding had cleared itself up. Without hearing what they were saying Emily had sat up in bed at ten minutes past midnight, listening to Langley arguing and Barney laugh-ing, and found it hard to get to sleep again.

She had been sure it was about Sian. Barney was up early this morning, out of the house before Langley came down, and Emily had asked him, 'What was all the fuss last night?'

'I was working late, and Langley doesn't trust me after dark with any self-respecting girl.'

He meant Sian, of course. Emily had said severely, 'I don't know as I'd trust you far. Now you behave yourself, because she's a nice girl, and your brother's very fond of her.'

She had comforted herself by reflecting that Sian had sense. Sian knew which brother was the marrying kind. But Langley had been depressed all through breakfast, and right from when they were boys Barney had had that bit of the devil in him that delighted in plaguing poor Langley.

Well, if there had been the makings of a quarrel Sian and Langley had got round it; they were obviously on comfort-able terms again. Langley pulled out Sian's chair for her, and she smiled up at him thanking him, and Emily said cheerfully, 'I got you a bit of fillet steak, seeing as you missed your breakfast.'

She served Langley with the fillet, herself and Sian with small neat pieces of rump steak. Then she said, 'They were nice duck eggs Mrs. Barker sent, I was wondering if you'd like to make a cake.'

Emily liked seeing Sian in the kitchen, not too much, not under her feet, but making the occasional cake or baking the odd pie. It was reassuring, like a mother checking on the housewifery potential of the girl her son might marry. The Hollis boys were Emily's family, Barney had chosen his own way of life, and Emily had no doubt there would always be someone around ready to cook for him; but she was glad that Sian had a light hand with the pastry and a deft touch with the leftovers.

Sian smiled at Langley, 'Can I have time off this afternoon to bake a cake?'

'Of course,' said Langley.

'Very kind of Mrs. Barker to send the eggs,' said Emily. 'She was telling me at W.I. that Phyllis and Gordon Wilkes are having a bungalow built on Woodgrange.'

Woodgrange Farm was owned by Phyllis's father, and as the wedding was off Sian hoped the bungalow was still at the planning stage. She said, 'Phyllis and Gordon aren't getting married. Phyllis told me this morning.' She chewed on her steak. 'Actually she came to see you, Langley, because she was feeling blue and you were always so understanding.'

She was teasing a little, although it was true, Langley was the kind of man you knew would be sympathetic and kind, and she was sorry for Phyllis. So was Langley. 'The poor girl,' he said. 'Was she very upset?'

'She'll get over it,' said Sian, and as Langley looked slightly reproachful, 'I'm not being unfeeling, she will. She said herself that it wouldn't have worked out.'

'So that's why she came round with the duck eggs,' said Emily. 'I hope we're not going to start that again.'

Emily sounded distinctly unsympathetic and Langley said, only half-smiling, 'You're a hard-hearted pair.'

'And you're too soft-hearted,' said Emily. 'Anybody can get round you.'

Well, it was an endearing failing. It was better than being too tough. Sian said, 'I'm glad you feel that way because I gave her brandy and sympathy, your best brandy. She went feeling much better, and slightly high.'

Langley smiled. 'Good,' he said. 'By the way, don't you

think we should celebrate your sale tonight? Go out some-where?'

This was how she had wanted him to be, seeing it as a lucky break, a bit of a joke and no more. She said, 'I'd love to, but I said I'd see this Ennerman man first.'

'Joss Ennerman's coming to you?' She hadn't had time to tell him that. Now she said,

'Barney said he was coming to talk to me.'

'I see!' The chill was creeping back. 'Would you object to me sitting in on the interview? After all, while you're work-ing in my gallery I'd like to know what Barney and Joss Ennerman are proposing for you.'

She said eagerly, 'Please do. I didn't ask him to come, you know. I've never heard of him before.'

'He has a reputation,' Langley admitted. There was an edgy silence, Emily looking from one to the other, while Sian groped desperately for a less controversial subject.

She came up with, 'Please may I buy the rocking horse?' Langley blinked, his train of thought jerked awry, and she went on, 'With the money I'm getting for the model, and a little bit more I could, couldn't I?'

'Well, yes. Why? Do you want it?'

Yes, she wanted it, or she wouldn't be buying it. She said, 'Very much.'

'I'll give it to you,' said Langley. 'You should have said you wanted it.'

That was sweet of him, but she tried to explain. 'You mustn't. It's quite a big sale, it would be nonsense, and I really would like to buy him; I'd like to do that.'

Langley couldn't afford gestures like making this kind of present. He shrugged now, 'As you like.'

'Do you think we could take him over to the stores as soon as you're through with your meal?'

'What's the hurry?'

She parted her lips to start telling how Barney had wanted it for Natalie but said that Sian could have it, but in the moment of choosing the words a warning buzzed in her brain. Langley had heard enough of Barney's goodwill gestures for one day. She said, 'What woman ever went shopping and didn't want to get the loot home? I want to see how he looks against the old oak beams.'

Langley smiled, 'You're a funny girl.'

They ate up quickly, while Emily warned them about indigestion, and then conveyed the rocking horse – a solid piece of work by any standards – into the van, to drive it down the high street to George and Fiona's doorstep. It was a very short ride, but better than carrying.

As they reached the stores Sian jumped out, and looked back up the road at the car they had just passed. She said, 'That was the Withingtons, they're stopping at the gallery.'

The Withingtons were good customers. They often dropped in if they were passing through the village, and almost always bought something. They were among the select few who could ring the bell when the notice said CLOSED and expect admission. Emily would open the door to them, but Sian or Langley would be needed from then on.

Sian said, 'Let's get the horse out, then you can get back. George and Fiona will help me get him upstairs.'

They lifted the horse from the van, and left him rocking on the pavement to the delight of the passers-by, while Langley reversed smartly into George McDade's entry and out again, and off back to the gallery to park behind the Withingtons' car.

The stores were still shut for the midday break, so Sian put her finger on the bell and kept it there, until the window immediately above – the kitchen window – opened, and Fiona stuck her head through. Sian called, 'Please will you let my horse in? He's too big for the side door.'

Fiona leaned out until she looked in danger of overbalancing, and was hauled back by George who announced that they would be right down.

The shop door opened, and George and Fiona came out. The rocking horse was a striking sight, with the sun gleaming on his new white coat and his pink spots. There was even the faintest of breezes ruffling his mane. He filled the pavement, which was a narrow one, and the need to move him was imperative. They opened the shop door as wide as it would go, and the three of them managed to half rock, half lift the horse through.

Fiona grinned, 'Don't tell me you rode him from the gallery.'

'Langley brought him for me in the van, but we saw the Withingtons arriving, so I made him dump me and get back to them. You know they bought that escritoire last time.'

'My goodness, yes,' said Fiona, who appreciated a good customer, and the need to hop to it when you saw one.

George closed the shop door, and slipped the lock on. There were still ten minutes to go before they were due to reopen, and they all looked at the horse in some awe. Even Sian, because it seemed so much bigger here in the low-ceilinged, well-stocked shop than it had done in the studio, George said, 'I reckon it's life-size, isn't it?'

'Nearly,' said Fiona breathlessly. She was as entranced with the horse as Sian had been. 'Isn't he beautiful?'

Sian said, 'Barney did tell you I was bringing him, didn't he?'

'Yes,' said George, 'but I didn't believe him, I thought he was rambling.'

'Now,' said Fiona briskly, 'we've got to get him upstairs.' There were two staircases up to Sian's room under the eaves, both narrow and winding, and the horse seemed to be getting bigger.

George said, 'You do realize we stand a very good chance of getting it wedged? I suppose it must come to pieces.' He squatted and peered at the rockers and whistled. 'But I'm darned if I can see where!'

'We're not carving him up,' said Fiona, with as much horror as though George had suggested dismembering a living animal, and he said, 'Believe it or not, it doesn't hurt 'em if you take off the rockers.'

'Well,' said Fiona grudgingly, 'not unless we absolutely have to. Only as a last resort if he does get stuck.'

'Shall I get Barney?' Sian suggested.

'He's got one good arm,' said George, 'let's have him.'

Barney was working, tapping away on his typewriter, and when she said, 'Hello,' he scowled at her. She said, 'I'm sorry to interrupt, but I've brought the rocking horse and he's in the shop and we've got to get him upstairs before the customers come.'

Barney went on scowling, but he got up and followed her out of Nelly's room and down the stairs to the ground floor. By now George and Fiona had manoeuvred the rocking horse to the bottom of the first flight of stairs where he towered magnificently. George sounded triumphant. 'I've measured him across the shoulders, you know we can just do it. It's all a matter of getting him round the corners.'

George was rubbing his hands, beginning to enjoy the challenge. Barney said, 'Can we take the rockers off?' and George said, 'If you do Fiona's going to report you to the R.S.P.C.A.'

'Don't be ridiculous,' said Fiona primly. 'I just think it would be a shame to start tearing him to pieces unless we have to.'

Sian said, 'This is an awful nuisance, isn't it? I didn't realize how heavy he was, nor how big.' She looked wistfully up, because the horse had a long way to go. She said, 'Maybe I'd better take him back to the studio. I can keep him there.'

'We can do it,' said George with immense confidence. 'If we can't get him up the stairs we'll take the window frame out and send him up on a crane.'

'Leave it till after midnight,' said Barney, 'and he'll fly in.'

He grinned at Sian and she said, 'No fooling, he's magic,' and Fiona giggled, and George said, 'Operation horse-lift starting now!'

Easy did it. They roped the rocking horse, and Barney took some of the weight from above, while George lifted, and the girls edged and coaxed and shrieked warnings and encouragement. They took a brief breather on the first floor, then did it all over again, up to the top floor under the eaves.

The horse was fairly co-operative. It didn't get wedged. By a hair's breadth it was eased round and up, and no one begrudged it a final fling at the very top of the stairs when the tip of a rocker caught a pile of aluminium saucepans and sent them flying and clattering.

A last heave and the horse rocked gently on the top floor outside Sian's room, and everyone stood back, a little dishevelled but smug with success.

'You know,' said George, 'I enjoyed that. It's a long time since I tried to get a horse up a spiral staircase.' He slapped its haunch and sent it rocking faster. 'Ah well,' he said, 'back to work.'

'Thank you,' said Sian. 'Thank you *very* much.'

George and Fiona hurried downstairs, they were five minutes late in opening, although nobody had rung the doorbell so presumably nobody cared. 'You'll have to stay now, Sian,' Fiona called as she went. 'You can't move away, because I don't think we can ever get him down again.'

'Come on,' said Barney. 'Let's get him over the threshold.'

Sian opened the door and pulled and pushed the horse in. She said, 'I had to bring him, I was scared you might change your mind if I didn't get him out of the gallery. You can't have him now,' she gloated, 'he's home.'

'Home and dry,' said Barney, 'and he goes a treat with the tin trays.'

'Doesn't he just? Oh, he *is* handsome! I'm sorry I dragged you away from your work, but it was an emergency, it won't happen again.'

'It had better not,' said Barney. He turned to go back through the archway to Nelly's room, and Sian asked,

'By the way, where am I supposed to be seeing Mr. Ennerman?'

'Here, about eight o'clock.'

The curtain swished behind Barney. She called again, 'Thank you,' and stroked the rocking horse once more before running all the way back to the gallery.

Langley had sold the Withingtons a petit-point footstool, a stirrup cup, and two pieces of ruby glass. They had gone by the time Sian returned and Langley was looking out for her. He asked, 'Did you manage all right?'

'Marvellously. They all gave me a hand, George and Fiona and Barney.'

'*Barney?*' His automatic reaction was alarm. 'Barney shouldn't be lifting weights. The doctor said—'

'There were four of us,' said Sian. 'He was all right. Oh, and Mr. Ennerman's coming to the stores to see me at about eight o'clock if you want to be there.'

'I do.' Langley was firm on that.

He was waiting with her when Joss Ennerman arrived. He had been there from half past seven, he and Sian drinking tea slowly, and talking about the auction and the day's business. Barney was still in Nell's room. Sometimes they heard his typewriter, at others the low murmur of his voice. From time to time Langley glanced at the curtain dividing the rooms, and once Sian said, 'It doesn't bother me. I can hardly hear the typewriter.'

'I can't see why he has to work in there,' said Langley.

'He isn't there *all* the time. Fiona says he goes out quite a lot.'

'He doesn't come home,' said Langley quietly. He listened to his brother's voice, straining to hear, but he wouldn't catch the words; Sian could have told him that. The curtain was too thick, the speaker too far away.

At a few minutes after eight Barney called, 'He's here, I'll let him in.' Barney would have seen the car arrive, he had the dais that gave him the advantage of being able to see through the window.

Looking at Langley Sian wished, not for the first time, that this hadn't started. She smiled and Langley smiled back, and she poured him out some more tea although he hadn't said he wanted any. She wondered whether she should go to what was after all her bed-sitter front door and open it for Mr. Ennerman, but she didn't feel Langley would appreciate anything that smacked of too much eagerness. So she stayed where she was, sitting on the divan, until Barney opened the door and walked in himself. Behind him came a man who practically filled the doorway, and then she got up and said, 'Good evening.'

Joss Ennerman was well over six foot, and deplorably overweight, with the face of a disillusioned cherub. When he smiled some of the weariness went and the cherub looked more hopeful. Sian said, 'Do sit down,' and he took one of the wickerwork armchairs that sagged alarmingly under him.

Langley sat down in the other chair, and Barney took one end of the divan. Sian was about to offer tea, realizing belatedly that she should have had something stronger to offer, but Joss Ennerman wasted no time on pleasantries. He said, 'Barney tells me you've only just started modelling. What have you been doing?'

He sounded accusing, as though she had frittered away the years of her youth, and she would have laughed if he had been a little less formidable. As it was she said weakly, 'Not a great deal, working for a living.'

He waved that away as no excuse at all, then he announced, 'I liked that figure. And the head.' He nodded approval. 'They had a strength about them. Yes, yes, I liked them.' He could have been awarding an order of merit, and inevitably Sian warmed towards him. 'You haven't done anything else?'

She said, 'I haven't got anything else. I didn't bother to have them fired. I only did them to amuse myself.'

'Very silly. Very wasteful.' He despaired of her and the whole human race, and she sat, rebuked, enjoying his larger-than-life performance, waiting for what was coming next. 'I hope,' he said sadly, 'you'll not do anything as stupid as that again.'

'I won't.'

'You'll let me know when you finish something else?'

'I will.

Langley said, 'There's a kiln at the gallery that Sian can use.'

'Excellent!' Ennerman turned to Langley as though he hadn't noticed him until now, and made what he plainly felt was a generous offer, 'And do you want to handle her work?'

Sian said quickly, 'It isn't right for the gallery. It would be out of place.' Langley didn't like her models and she didn't want him bothered with them. Instinct told her they should be kept out of sight and out of mind as much as possible, where Langley was concerned.

He seemed to agree. He said, 'I'm sure Mr. Ennerman can command a wider market than I can. By all means take advantage of it.'

'I'm not going to be producing enough for it to matter much, am I?' She smiled apologetically at Ennerman. 'I am fairly busy, this will be very much of a sideline.'

He didn't smile back. 'Busy?' he said. 'Busy doing what?'

'I work in the Little Gallery.'

'You mean you serve in the shop.' Literally, put like that, yes. She said, 'Yes, and I enjoy it, and I intend to go on doing it.'

She wished he would sit still in the wickerwork chair instead of shifting forward every time he was stressing a point, because she would hate it to collapse beneath him. He leaned forward now and said emphatically, 'Get your priorities in order, Miss Rowan. I'm not saying you've the makings of genius, but from the little – the very little – I have seen of your work, I think you have enough talent to justify taking it more seriously than this.'

He was the expert. His valuation carried authority, and her first reaction was delight. Her second was Langley, who was her top priority, and loving Langley meant serving in the shop, encouraging his painting, baking cakes and typing letters. She looked at Langley, speaking to Joss Ennerman, and said, 'Thank you, Mr. Ennerman, I'll let you know if I have anything else I think you might be interested in. And thank you again for selling the figure for me.'

Barney stood up. He had said nothing till now, and now

he said, 'Right, that seems to cover it. Come on, Joss, I'll buy you a drink.'

Ennerman hesitated for a moment, then got to his feet with remarkable bounce considering his bulk and how far down into the chair he had sunk. He looked at the rocking horse. 'Very impressive,' he said. 'How did you get it up the stairs?'

'It wasn't easy,' said Barney, and Sian laughed,

'It was easier than I'd expected.' She went to the door with them, keeping the laughter going. 'Good-bye,' she said.

'Good night.' Joss Ennerman held her hand in a surprisingly light grip; she was expecting a bone-crusher. 'Good night,' he said to Langley, and looked again at Sian. 'Remember – get those priorities in order.'

She said gaily, 'I think I do have them in order.'

'Hmmm,' said Ennerman, and he followed Barney down the narrow winding stairs, holding the rail and stepping with care.

Sian leaned over the top, and was thankful to see him reach street level without mishap. Then she turned back to Langley. 'He's a bit overpowering, isn't he?'

Langley's own smile was wary, a shadow smile. 'He certainly is. He seems to feel you're wasting your time, working in the gallery.'

She dismissed that opinion. 'How can it be time wasted doing something I love doing? Whatever Joss Ennerman says, anything else will always be a sideline.'

'I'm glad.' His eyes showed gratitude for reassurance. 'I don't want anything to be more important to you than the things I can give you.'

She said softly, 'Nothing is.'

Barney obviously felt at ease with Joss Ennerman, but Langley, less assured himself, found the big man's domineering manner as wearing as a force eight gale. He said thoughtfully, 'I sometimes wonder if Ennerman isn't a great big phoney. He's got money, and half a dozen galleries. Modern art is his line, but just how much of what he says is sincere and how much is part of the act I wouldn't know.'

'You think he was putting on an act for me?' She couldn't see why he should take the trouble, she hoped he wasn't, and Langley said,

'No, of course you have talent. It's just that Joss Ennerman always strikes me as a sort of circus act.'

'He'd make a good ringmaster.' In top hat, red coat, white breeches, cracking a long, long whip, but not hurting. Cracking his whip for the fun of it.

They didn't go out to celebrate Sian's sale after all. It seemed too late now to start looking for somewhere with a festive air, so they stayed where they were and listened to a play on the radio. Langley went home about ten o'clock, and Sian washed her hair and sat on the floor and combed it dry in front of one bar of the electric fire.

She heard the footsteps and called, 'Who is it?' at the knock on the door.

'Barney.'

'What do you want?'

'Talk. About two minutes of it.'

'All right.' As he came in she said, 'I know it isn't after midnight yet, but don't go out of your way to tell Langley you came back here. It irritates him. What do you want to talk about?'

She went on combing her hair, peering at him through it. He said, 'Joss wants me to impress on you that you must go on with your modelling. He doesn't often get excited, but he thinks you're good.'

She said, 'Tell me about him. Is he an artist himself?'

'He hoped to be. He was just starting, in Paris, when he put his hand through the glass of a swing-door and cut the tendons. His right hand is all but helpless, and Joss isn't the man to settle for producing second-best work. So he helps young artists instead. He's no philanthropist, he makes a very comfortable living, but everything in his galleries is exciting and most of it's good.'

'You wouldn't call him a phoney?'

Barney grinned, 'Only to his face. If you mean – is he a

phoney? No, he isn't. He's real enough, flamboyant perhaps, but he bleeds.'

'Do you bleed?'

It might have been chance that he glanced at the rocking horse. The rocking horse . . . Natalie . . . 'Less than most,' he said. 'Where will you be working?'

'Here,' she was decided on that, 'and don't make too much of it, please. I don't want Langley to feel—'

'God forbid,' said Barney. 'You send 'em off in a plain van, love, after dark.'

She tossed her damp hair back. Barney wasn't used to worrying about anyone else's feelings, but when you loved somebody surely you should consider them, and Langley didn't like Joss Ennerman and he wouldn't enjoy being reminded that Sian was working for Joss now as well as for himself. 'Good night,' she said stiffly.

'Good night,' said Barney, and went out laughing at her. She allowed herself the childish gesture of grimacing at the closing door.

Langley didn't ask and she didn't tell him. No more was said about her using the old kiln either, but next day she started work on a head of Joss Ennerman. A little because the idea amused her, but mostly because that cherubic face had a wealth of character. No one asked about it and no one saw it, and she did it at night, after work, for the best part of a week. She had done that head of Barney in hours, but now she took pains, using her mind as much as the instinctive skill of her hands.

Barney was working too, on his play. She only saw him a couple of times that week, once fleetingly at breakfast, once when she came home and passed him on the stairs going out. She said, 'How's life?'

'Well in hand,' he said. They smiled briefly on each other, and she went up and he went down.

It was an uneventful week. Barney bothered nobody, except Emily and Langley who knew he was working too hard. Sian heard the typewriter several evenings, and looked through the curtains once to ask if he'd like some coffee. He said, 'No,' adding, 'Thank you' as an afterthought, making her so flagrant an intruder that she vowed never again. He could brew his own coffee!

Sales in the gallery were slightly higher than the same week last year. Langley did a little more of Deniston Crag, and Phyllis Barker visited the gallery twice.

She came the first time, she said, to see Sian again and apologize for having drunk the brandy. She was afraid she must have made an awful fool of herself because even after the walk home she had felt light-headed. Sian said, 'You were fine, of course you were,' but Phyllis remained doubtful if grateful.

'It was nice of you anyway,' said Phyllis. 'It certainly cheered me up, I was feeling *so* miserable.'

'Are you feeling better now?' Sian asked. The engagement hadn't been mended. Emily had had that news since from several sources, and Phyllis said forlornly,

'I suppose so.'

Langley was in the display rooms, showing some customers Victorian fashion plates that could be framed if selected, when Phyllis came in. She had asked for Sian, and Langley had said, 'Do go through.'

So Phyllis had walked into the studio, where Sian was copying another miniature, and said, 'Hello. I just had to come and apologize for making such a fool of myself on Monday.'

Langley, through with his customers, joined them, and Sian watched the colour rise in Phyllis's fair betraying skin. Although he deliberately held back from the talk, and got himself immersed in several phone calls, just being in the same room with him was putting stars in Phyllis's eyes.

She stayed as long as she could, talking about the miniature and the painting and the weather, until Sian said, 'It's been nice seeing you again, but you have picked a rather busy time.'

Then she flushed even deeper, and stammered her apologies, and Sian felt like someone who has thrown a small puppy out in the snow as Phyllis scurried out of the gallery into the sunshine.

Langley was gently reproving. 'You were a bit short with her, weren't you?'

She said defensively, 'She still has a king-size crush on you.'

'Oh, I don't think so.' It was three years since he had met Phyllis Barker at every turn, her round face earnest and adoring. She had been seventeen then, and she knew they were laughing at her, and that although Langley Hollis was kind and talked to her she only embarrassed him. It hadn't been funny for Phyllis. One night she had gone down to the river, and wept there alone because she hadn't the courage to die and she didn't know how she was going to go on living. After that she had somehow found the courage to keep away.

She was pretty, and there were boy-friends. Gordon Wilkes was her parents' choice, because he was a farmer like her father and would take the place of the son they'd longed for and never had. Her father was building them a bungalow, and Gordon was coming to work at Woodgrange.

Everybody was pleased about that. It couldn't have been more convenient, Gordon the youngest of three sons, no farm of his own and no prospects of one. Big and strong and healthy and uncomplicated.

But in the last few weeks a panic had been building up in Phyllis. Emily described her as a silly little thing, and that was the general impression. It seemed to Phyllis that all her life she had been trying desperately to make people like her, over-eager, trotting at heels. She knew it, but she couldn't help it.

Gordon had said on Sunday night, 'For God's sake, Phyl, you're worse than an old woman!' She had been urging him to wear a scarf. It wasn't cold, she had put the scarf on him simply because it was hanging in the hall and they were going out in an open car and it could turn cold later. He had torn it off again, and instead of getting into his sports car they had ended up standing beside it, while Gordon's frustration burst bounds. The farm wasn't worth it, nothing was worth it, she was driving him daft.

She had known this was coming. She had read the signs, and it was almost a relief. She had turned and run for the bus stop, and Gordon following her had been glad to see her catch a bus. Surprised too, for they rarely arrived on cue.

He had phoned Woodgrange several times since, on his own parents' insistence, but he had breathed more freely hearing that Phyl didn't want to speak to him. She was a nice kid, but a lifetime with her wasn't for him.

She had of course seen Langley occasionally in the last three years – it was a small village – and every time she saw him her heart flipped. Even walking past the gallery could do it. Now she was making a fool of herself again. They'd all be laughing and talking. Langley Hollis was going to marry Sian Rowan, almost everyone said so, and Phyllis walked briskly, head up, lips tucked into a small social smile, aching with misery.

Phyllis had no luck at all. She didn't expect it, and she wasn't surprised when she next looked in at the gallery to hear that Langley was away for the afternoon, calling on another dealer who had what might be just the grandfather clock Langley was trying to find for one of his own customers.

She had her reason for calling pat – the painting of Denniston Crag. She wanted to know how much Langley was asking for it, and Sian said, 'I'm afraid I don't know, and he won't be back for a while. May we phone you?'

'Yes, please,' said Phyllis. She looked at the picture again, as though it was a Turner sunset, and then at Sian's miniature. 'You're very talented too, aren't you?' she said.

'Thank you,' said Sian; what else was there to say? The ringing of the shop door bell was more welcome than ever just then, because it meant that Phyllis followed her out of the studio and said,

'Good-bye for now,' and Sian said,

'Good afternoon, can I help you?' to the customer.

When the customer left it was a few minutes after half-five and Sian clicked down the latch and turned the

CLOSED notice, then she went back to the studio. The miniature was almost done, she might as well work on and finish it. And stay and hear if Langley had been successful.

The bell rang again as the door was opened, this time by someone with a key, and she called, 'Langley? I'm in here.'

Barney came in. 'Sorry,' he said, 'wrong wavelength. Working overtime?'

'Just finishing this.' She was sitting, with the miniature before her, copying from a faded sepia photograph of a bearded man, and the instructions that had come with it: Eyes blue, Hair mid-brown.

He said, 'There's a storm coming.'

'Is there?' It wouldn't affect her much, with only a two-minute dash needed to get her home. The sky had been overcast enough all afternoon for the electric light to be on in the studio, but she was managing the miniature.

Barney said, 'He's a rakish-looking feller.'

'Was, I should think. It's dated 1901.' She picked up the photograph and held it at arm's length. 'The eyes are flat, the light faded years ago. I'll have to put it back, won't I? And that's a liberty, because I don't know what was behind that face.'

'I shouldn't let it worry you. I don't suppose the ones who want the miniature knew either.'

'Probably not.' She put the photograph back on the table, and turned to look at Barney again. He looked tired. She said, 'They say you're overworking.'

'The sooner it's done the sooner I'm away.'

She snapped, 'Not if you set yourself back a couple of months in the process.'

'You're in a carping mood.'

'Yes,' she was. She said, 'Well, at least ask me if I've started on another model.'

'Have you?'

'I have, and it's no good at all.'

She had come to that conclusion last night, late. It was

still clay, moulded like a face, but nothing inside. Like the photograph she was copying it told no secrets. Fiona, who had seen it several times, said that it was marvellous, but Fiona was a friend and no critic.

Once Barney really plunged into his own work Sian had known that he would have no time and no interest left for hers. Still, having started the whole thing going, she felt he might have spared the odd five minutes.

She couldn't talk to Langley about it. If she did Langley would say, 'Why bother if you're not enjoying it, and you don't feel you're producing anything worth while?'

Barney said, 'We all get that feeling. Right now I want to tear the whole damn thing up, and start again from square one.'

'You do?'

'A right load of old rubbish it's turning out to be.'

Perhaps he *had* started work too soon after the accident. She pointed out, 'Everybody's been trying to tell you you should go slow for a while,' and he came back with the scathing weariness of one addressing an idiot bigot,

'I'm practically immobilized, for gawd's sake. You can't go much slower than that, even in this town.'

'You're deliberately misunderstanding me. You can do too much sitting still when it's brain work.'

'Listen!' He came round to face her. 'I was physically smashed in that crash, not mentally retarded.'

'I know that.' She sounded as exasperated as he did. Reason was on her side. She was the one talking sense. 'But if your work isn't up to scratch it's because you're not, isn't it?'

'No.' He disclaimed all responsibility. 'It's because my characters have turned bloody-minded.'

She remembered the head she was trying to model, and began to smile. 'So has my lump of clay. It had me in tears last night, beating my head on the carpet. The rocking horse thought I'd gone mad.'

His smile lit from hers, and they laughed together. Then he said, 'I bet these never had you in tears.' He touched the

124

miniature. A competent job of work, rating no tears. She didn't weep easily, but last night that clay had had her weeping.

She said, 'True. What can I do about it?'

'Well, I'm going for a good long walk.'

'The rain's starting.'

Summer rain, spattering on the big northern window. 'All the better,' he said.

She went to the table with the typewriter, and picked up the pair of white gloves she had noticed just before he came in. 'If you're not going anywhere in particular you could take Phyllis Barker's gloves back for her. She wants to buy Langley's picture, and she left her gloves behind.'

'We'll both take them,' said Barney. 'You come as well.'

'All right.' She had no coat, but it was oppressively warm in spite of the rain, it could end in thunder. A walk in the rain would be pleasant and Woodgrange Farm wasn't far. She put Phyllis's nylon gloves in her handbag, cleaned her paintbrushes, and left the faded sepia photograph, and the miniature with its flesh tints and its blue eyes, side by side. 'Come on, then,' she said.

Barney had wandered to the easel and Deniston Crag. That was where Langley was going to ask Sian again to marry him, and where she was going to say yes. If Phyllis knew that she wouldn't want the picture. Sian sighed for her, 'Poor Phyllis!'

'Why?' Barney followed her out of the studio. 'It isn't that bad and Langley's bound to sell it to her cheap.'

He was being obtuse on purpose and she wasn't rising to the bait. She said sweetly, 'So he is. As you get your share of the profits of this place you should be grateful I'm here to curb some of Langley's generosity.'

'I am.' He sounded as though his cut from the Little Gallery kept him from starving. 'It's a great comfort to me to know that when Langley prices the goods you nip along later upping them ten per cent.'

'That is an idea.'

She closed the shop door and it locked behind them,

'Does it bother you that Langley has this odd fixation about giving the customer a fair deal?'

'It does. Still, we're none of us perfect, are we? That's why Langley needs a mercenary-minded wife.'

They were walking along the high street, and the rain was fine as sea spray. Sian could almost imagine it tasted salt on her lips. She said, 'I am not mercenary-minded.'

'Don't tell me I've made a mistake, and fixed him up with the wrong girl.'

There were fewer people than usual about, and those that were in the high street were walking quickly to get in out of the rain. Several spoke as they passed. Sian said, after one brief exchange, giving Barney her attention again, 'You have fixed nobody up with anybody. You may have given things a slight starter push, but Langley and I are managing nicely for ourselves, thank you. You keep your mind on your fiction characters. You can't even control them, it seems.'

'All I need,' said Barney, 'is a short breathing space, then I'll show them who's boss. Do we take the spinney or the road?'

You could get to Woodgrange Farm either way. The road would have been more sensible, the rain was dripping through the trees and had turned the ground to spongy softness. But the woods were prettier, and Sian said, 'This way, please.'

Barney went over the stile, and held out a hand for her. She took it, steadying her climb over, and asked, 'What *is* the play about?'

'It's a TV script.' He loosed her as soon as she stood on the path, and walked just ahead, along the narrow track between the silver birches. 'About a policeman who left the force after obtaining the conviction of a murderer. He had doubts himself after the conviction. The man's daughter wants her father's innocence proved, and asks the ex-copper to help.'

'Was he innocent?'

'No.'

'Oh!' She demanded of Barney's back, 'Then what's the

point of it?' and he shrugged.

'At the moment that eludes me too. Now let's discuss your problems. What are you modelling?'

'A head of Joss Ennerman.' She felt like an Oriental wife, five paces behind, until Barney stepped into the rough grass to walk beside her, leaving the track.

'Very nice,' he said. 'Although unless Joss fancies it for himself I shouldn't think there's much of a market for Joss Ennerman heads.'

A heavy raindrop plopped from the leaf above her, tickling her cheek like a caress. She smiled, 'You see, that proves I'm not mercenary-minded.' She breathed in the cool wet air. 'This is splendid for clearing the head. Do you do much walking when you're stuck for ideas?'

'A fair amount.'

She put her foot on a mud patch, slippery smooth as ice, and it shot from beneath her, so that she would have gone flat if he hadn't grabbed her. 'Not bad for a one-armed catch,' he said.

She was breathless, but she laughed. 'I'll give you this, there's nothing wrong with your reflexes!'

They walked on, his arm still around her, casually, because it was easier to walk this way with the path so narrow and so slippery. They walked quietly for a few minutes, then she took up the talk again. 'For inspiration the country's got the edge on your old city streets.'

'Oh, I don't know. You've seen one cow, you've seen them all.'

Over their heads the sky showed dull silver through the pattern of leaves and branches. She said, 'The woods are beautiful.'

'But not so interesting as the human race.'

'You think not?'

'Try looking behind the faces sometimes, there's your jungle.'

She said, 'The woods are safe. Who wants to swap them for a jungle?'

Jungles were cruel and turbulent places. It was better to

be safe. There was no reason why she shouldn't walk with Barney in the rain, and the prickling of her skin was because she was wet through and beginning to chill. It had nothing to do with warning of danger.

She said lightly, 'And you'd have to be a mind-reader to see behind the faces.'

'See if you are.' He turned her so that she looked up at him. Langley was the handsome one, Barney – three years younger – looked older. His was the experienced face that had seen and been heaven-knows-what and heaven-knows-where. You'd need to be a genuine telepathist to learn anything he was trying to hide.

It was probably wetter under the trees now than out in the open. The leaves were brimming over with rain, and it cascaded down in shining little waterfalls.

She said unsteadily, 'I can tell your fortune if that will do. You're going to catch pneumonia.'

'Not me,' he said, 'I can't spare the time.'

'Well, I shall.' She was shivering. 'I hope Phyllis Barker's got a fire going.'

She wanted to move and quickly. Looking up at Barney it was natural enough that she should wonder how it would be if he kissed her. Not a good idea, she was convinced. A crazy lunatic risk to take.

But he was going to kiss her, and if she jumped away like a scalded cat he'd know she was scared. She closed her eyes and felt his lips on her cheek, cool and light as the rain.

Then he said, 'You'll not get pneumonia either. Two minutes to Woodgrange, and you can sit on top of the stove and dry out.'

'Lovely,' she said. She laughed, and they began to run, and she held down a strange and tiny pang that could almost have been disappointment.

CHAPTER SEVEN

WOODGRANGE was a good-sized and prosperous farm, although now, grey stone under the grey skies, it looked chill and slightly forbidding. The rain was coming hard and they ran for the front door, and Barney knocked the heavy horse-shoe door knocker while Sian leaned against the wall and tried to get her breath back.

She was a sight, her dress sticking to her, her hair lank and dripping, and Phyllis, opening the door, had every excuse for astonishment. 'Oh!' exclaimed Phyllis. 'You *are* wet!'

Sian said, 'We brought your gloves back.'

Phyllis was horrified. 'Oh, you shouldn't have done. It didn't matter. Any time would have done. You never came out in this, just to bring my gloves?'

'Not entirely,' said Barney.

They were still standing in the rain, and Phyllis collected her wits and opened the door wider. 'Do come in. Come and get dry.'

The hall had an oak-block floor, and a couple of Persian rugs. The oak blocks gleamed with high polish, and Sian guessed that the back door was used more than the front door. No one marched through here in farmer's boots. She felt guilty at the footsteps she and Barney were leaving. She skirted the Persian rugs, but even after a vigorous scrape on the front door mat her shoes were still damp and muddy.

Phyllis hovered for a moment at the open door of the sitting room, then she said, 'It's warmer in the kitchen, and the fire's in there.'

'Oh, the kitchen, please,' said Sian. She could see that the chairs in the sitting-room were covered with pale blue silk, and they followed Phyllis down the hall into the kitchen.

There was a good fire burning and a spicy smell in the air, and Mrs. Barker at the stove stirring a pan of some sort of preserve, and watching the kitchen door to see who was coming.

She looked as shocked as Phyllis, and nearly lost her wooden spoon in the preserve in her anxiety to get Sian to the fire. 'Oh, my goodness, you are wet! It has turned into a nasty day, hasn't it? Come and get to the fire.'

'They brought my gloves back,' said Phyllis, determined to take the blame. 'I left them at the gallery.'

Mrs. Barker breathed deep, leaving things unsaid but looking hard at Phyllis. She apologized for her daughter, 'Oh dear, you shouldn't have bothered bringing them back in this.'

'It wasn't this bad when we started,' Sian assured her. 'It was just a drizzle then, but it's only summer rain, it won't hurt.'

She stood in front of the fire and steamed a little. Barney was every bit as wet, but black slacks and sweater didn't show it so much. She was conscious of the way her dress was clinging, and when Mrs. Barker said, 'You should get out of that dress,' she was inclined to agree.

'I'll get you something,' Phyllis offered.

'Would you?'

'You come with me.'

Sian went with Phyllis, and towelled herself down in the bathroom while Phyllis laid out a small selection of possibles on the bed in her bedroom. Sian was taller and thinner, and the first dress she put on had both girls smiling. She ended with a sweater and skirt, and as she pulled the sweater over her head Phyllis asked hopefully, 'Do you often go out with Barney?'

Sian shook her hair loose. 'No,' she said. Phyllis's train of thought was obvious, and it would be cruel to let her build on it. She went on, 'I felt like a walk and so did he. That's all. Barney has a girl, you know.'

Phyllis Barker knew. With most of the local female population she had watched Natalie on television and heard all about the week-end she had spent down here. But it would have been fabulous if Sian had been interested in Barney, not in Langley.

She said, 'Barney Hollis is quite famous, isn't he? He's the only celebrity we've ever had in this village. Well, it's a small place, isn't it, and they're not a very go-ahead lot, are they?' She chattered gaily on, a little worried frown revealing everything she was trying to hide. 'I think he's fascinating,' she said, 'don't you? And that car crash that brought him down here has probably made him appreciate a bit of home life.'

It would have amused Barney, to hear Phyllis Barker trying to sell him to Sian. It was sad to Sian, because Phyllis was transparent and asking for heartache. Sian said, 'Barney can't wait to get away from here, and when he does I don't suppose we'll see him again for months, years maybe. He doesn't appreciate home life and he never will.'

She smiled as she spoke to show that it wouldn't hurt her, but her voice was rueful because it was hard on Langley. She said, 'I suppose you and Gordon—?' Phyllis shook her head. 'I'm sorry,' said Sian.

'It doesn't matter,' said Phyllis. 'I don't blame him a bit. He can't help being the way he is.'

'What way is he?' Sian wasn't sure she should have asked that, but it was an intriguing point.

Phyllis said, 'Oh, he just doesn't understand me. You can't talk to him about anything that matters, just the farm and football and that car of his.'

Very healthy, very dull; anyhow, soon Sian and Langley would be announcing their engagement, and then Phyllis would realize that Langley, no matter how understanding, was no longer available.

Sian tugged gently at the sweater, trying to lengthen it a little, and said, 'Thank you for these. We'd better be getting back, Langley will be wondering where we are.'

Phyllis smiled. She did it dreamily so that it was probably less at Sian that at Langley's name, and Sian wondered whether she should say here and now, 'Langley and I are getting married.' But she lacked the callousness, or the courage. She knew that Phyllis's lips would tremble, and her eyes would swim with tears, and she simply did not feel up to handling the situation.

She picked up her damp dress instead, and they went back downstairs to the kitchen.

Barney was drinking whisky, and telling Mr. and Mrs. Barker some tale that had them laughing. You could hear their laughter half-way down the stairs, and Mr. Barker was wiping his eyes as the girls walked in and making appreciative mirthful noises. Still laughing, he got up to offer Sian a glass of whisky.

She said, 'No, thank you, I really think we should be getting back.'

Mrs. Barker was spooning her preserve, tomato chutney, into rows of pots, and it was her suggestion that somebody should drive them home.

'That's all right,' said Barney. Sian would have liked a lift, the rain was still pouring down. She was glad when Mr. Barker said, 'Of course you can't walk back in this,' and Phyllis offered,

'I'll take you, you brought my gloves. It isn't more than a minute or two by car, but it's far enough to get you wet through again.'

Mrs. Barker presented Sian with a jar of chutney, very hot and to be held carefully because it hadn't set; and they wrapped up Sian's damp dress for her. They made her drink a cup of tea. She was anxious to get back now, Langley would surely be home, and a short walk with Barney was one thing but an evening out with him was another.

Mr. Barker and Barney looked as though they might well have made a night of it, and Mrs. Barker and Phyllis were urging Sian to stay to tea. She settled for a cup of tea without, she hoped, sounding too ungracious, and Barney got up reluctantly when she did.

He was listening to Mr. Barker's account of his troubles this year with the gipsy pea-pickers, and Mrs. Barker had finished her chutney spooning and was adding an occasional word.

Only Phyllis seemed ready to go, and Barney eyed the

two standing girls and got up slowly. 'You come round again,' said Mr. Barker heartily. 'Any time at all.'

'Thank you,' said Barney, 'I will.'

He and Sian got into Phyllis's shooting brake, and she drove them back to the gallery. As she parked she said, as though the thought had just struck her, 'I think I'll come in. If Langley's back I'd like to know what he wants for the painting.'

'By all means,' said Barney.

Sian felt that she would do better to wait. A painting by Langley Hollis, after he was firmly committed to another woman, was not going to do Phyllis's morale much good; but the painting wasn't finished so Phyllis could always change her mind.

They all got out of the car, and Barney opened the gallery door. If Langley was home yet he didn't come to meet them when the bell over the shop door rang in the house and the studio. They walked the length of the display room and Sian looked into the studio – Langley wasn't there, and neither was his briefcase, so it looked as though he was not back yet.

Barney had gone into the hall, while Phyllis stood between the two doors, undecided which to step through, waiting for someone to tell her.

They heard Barney shout, and ran towards his voice, towards the kitchen. Emily lay there, sprawled in horribly crooked fashion, a tumbled chair and a smashed electric light bulb showing what had happened. Barney was on his knees, and Phyllis screamed, and Sian went down too, kneeling beside Barney to touch Emily's chalk-white face and thank God it was warm.

Her eyes were closed. For a moment of sick terror Sian had thought her dead. Barney got up. He said, 'Don't move her, I'll get the doctor.'

'Is she—?' Phyllis croaked, as she gulped for breaths between the screams, and Barney said,

'She's unconscious. Shut up.'

He spoke viciously enough to check Phyllis's screams and

133

she began to whimper instead, and crept towards Sian, her eyes wide and terrified on Emily.

Sian put a cushion under Emily's head, and began to chafe her hands. She didn't know what good that would do, except reassure her if she regained consciousness that she was no longer alone.

How long had she lain here? It could have been for hours. Sian had been in the studio all afternoon. When Barney had come he had gone straight into the studio, and they had both left without looking in on Emily. She could have been here from just after lunch. Lying here, calling even. With all the doors closed no one would have heard. Usually Sian did look in, but this afternoon she had felt depressed – that wretched model was plaguing her – she hadn't felt like chatting.

Barney came back and Sian raised her head. 'Did you get him?'

'He's taking surgery. He'll be right along.' He had brought a coat and he put it over Emily. Phyllis was sobbing jerkily – the shock had given her mild hysteria – and Barney said impatiently, 'Be quiet or get out, one or the other.'

Sian said, 'Go and let the doctor in, please, Phyllis. And Langley should be here soon too. Go and open the door for Langley.'

Phyllis fled. They heard her bump into something in the hall, probably the small table. It went over with a crash, and they heard Phyllis, still weeping, stop either to set it straight or gather up the pieces.

Dr. Murray was at the front door almost as soon as Phyllis reached it. Emily opened her eyes as he came into the kitchen. Barney had been talking to her, quietly. 'It's all right, Emmy love, it's all right.' She looked up at Barney, her voice so faint it was almost inaudible.

'I was calling you. I was calling for you.'

'I'm here, Emmy. And the doctor's here.'

'When did this happen?' Dr. Murray asked.

'I don't know,' said Barney.

One look and Dr. Murray said, 'We'll be needing that stretcher. They won't be long.' Emily had closed her eyes again, but her fingers held Barney's. Even when the pain-killing injection should have sent her back into insensibility she still clutched him.

The nearest hospital was Ivy House, about five miles away, and an ambulance was at the gallery while Dr. Murray was still conducting his examination. He didn't like what he was finding. Without X-rays and proper equipment and conditions he couldn't say with certainty the extent of the harm that slipping chair had done to Emily's no-longer-supple body. But he could see that she had a compound fracture of the hip, and at Emily's age that was enough to cripple her.

When the ambulance arrived he went with Barney. On the doorstep Sian said, 'I'll wait for Langley. You will ring me, won't you?'

'I'll ring,' said Barney. He looked grim and haggard. . . . 'I was calling you,' Emily had said, 'I was calling for you. . . .' Sian wondered if he was remembering when his father had called, and had died unanswered, and an almost unbearable pity took possession of her.

She said, 'Barney,' the longing to find the right words making her stammer so that no words came, and she put a hand on his arm and bit her lip. 'I – I—'

He shook off her hand. 'For God's sake,' he said, 'don't you go hysterical on me too. Wait for Langley for that.'

The pity for him went, and without it she was cool and articulate again. She said, 'I don't go hysterical on anyone. Please ring as soon as there's any news.'

She watched him get into the ambulance, and she watched it drive away. By now, of course, the neighbours were out. Everyone knew. Fiona came running down the road as Sian stood there, and said, 'Is it bad?'

'The doctor seems to think so. She fell off a chair. She was changing the light bulb.' It had been dark all afternoon, Emily could have tried to put in a new bulb any time. Sian went on, 'I keep telling myself I should have gone into the kitchen, at least before I finished for the night.'

'Do you always?'

135

'No, but sometimes. Oh, *why* didn't I do it today?'

'Come on home,' said Fiona.

'I can't, I've got to wait for Langley; and Barney's going to phone here.'

'All right,' said Fiona, 'I'll come and sit with you.'

There was no shortage of comfort. The Little Gallery seemed to be full of people waiting for news of Emily. George went looking for Langley; he was easy to find, he was still with the dealer he had gone to visit.

Sian stayed at the gallery, taking the call from Barney that came just before ten o'clock. A compound fracture of the hip, needing immediate surgery, and now Emily was under sedation, and he and Langley were coming back.

She put down the phone and told them all, and then they went home – most of them shaking their heads and murmuring about Emily's age and this being a long job at its best.

Fiona waited with Sian, and Phyllis Barker hadn't gone home. She had pulled herself together, and was laying a meal on the kitchen table when the door bell sounded.

It was easy to see which brother cared most for Emily. Barney looked grim still, but Langley was the one in real distress. Both Sian and Phyllis went into the hall, hearing the bell, and Langley passed them as though he hardly saw them.

Phyllis ran after him into the kitchen. Sian paused for a moment to look at Barney. 'She isn't—?'

'No,' he said. 'As I told you, she's under sedation. She was badly shocked, of course, and it's a bad break.'

'But she will be all right?'

'They don't know.'

Langley was sitting with his head in his hands. Beside him Phyllis was beginning to weep again, the tears welling in her eyes; and Sian touched his shoulder gently, promising. 'She will be all right.'

He looked up then, his face drawn, his eyes dark. 'All she's done for us, and she lies there like that, and no one knows or cares. I shouldn't have been out, I should have been around.'

'How could you know? How could anybody know?' It was useless to torture yourself because of something you might have done, but she could understand that the thought of Emily, his mother since he was three years old, lying in agony hour after hour, would be vivid and terrible in his mind.

He said, 'Why didn't you look in before you went home?'

'I don't always, you know that.' Perhaps two nights out of five, and not tonight.

Langley looked at Barney. They had come back together from the hospital, but Sian felt they hadn't talked. Surely Langley hadn't driven the car. He looked dazed, as though he was still in shock. 'Where were you?' he asked Barney.

'Sian and I went for a walk, to Woodgrange.'

'Why?'

Barney said quietly, 'Why not?' You don't need reasons for a walk, any more than for a cup of coffee or for picking up a newspaper, a small ordinary everyday thing.

Phyllis said tremulously, 'They brought my gloves back, I left—' and Langley's voice drowned hers in passionate self-hating.

'If Emily dies because I wasn't there I shall never forgive myself as long as I live!'

Sian wondered if he would forgive her and Barney. Phyllis pleaded, 'Please have something to eat,' but no one bothered to answer that and Barney said,

'Better get some rest.'

There was no point in the girls staying any longer. There would be no more news until tomorrow, and that would have to be faced soon enough, but Langley echoed Sian's thoughts. 'How do you expect to rest tonight?'

'I don't know,' said Barney, 'but I'm certainly going to try.'

It would be Langley who would stay sleepless. Barney was worried, he was grieving for Emily too, but some time within the next few hours he would sigh and sleep. Langley would see the dawn rise.

Fiona said, 'I think we'd all better try,' and Sian bent to kiss Langley.

'Good night, darling,' she said. 'There'll be good news in the morning, you see.'

'You really think so?' He knew she couldn't know, but he was grateful for her pretence.

She nodded. She remembered Emily when Barney was in that car crash, saying all the time, 'He'll be all right,' and he had been. Maybe it would work again, for Emily. She said, 'I'm sure of it.'

As she and Fiona walked through the darkened street towards the stores Fiona said, 'It's dreadful for Langley. Emily's done such a lot for him, and now he feels he failed her when she needed him most.'

'He couldn't help it.'

'Of course he couldn't.' Fiona opened the side door, and they went up the narrow creaking stairs. 'But if anything does happen to Emily he's going to take it very hard. If only—'

'If only I'd gone into the kitchen,' Sian said, 'instead of going off with Barney.'

'Yes,' said Fiona, 'I suppose so. Come in and have a drink.'

'I think I'll go up to my room,' said Sian, and Fiona went into her own sitting-room, where George was waiting, wishing she hadn't said that just now. It hadn't been tactful, it had been like thinking aloud. She said to George, 'Barney and Langley are back.'

'I know,' he said, 'I brought them back. Langley wasn't fit to drive and Barney couldn't.'

So George had been at the hospital too. She asked, 'What did they say? I know Emily's broken her hip, but did you hear any more?'

He was smoking his pipe; he didn't do that much, only when life became more of a strain than usual. 'She fell just before half-past five, when Sian would be closing the gallery. She said she prayed for someone to come in. She lay on the flagstones shivering, and she lost a fair amount of blood, and now pneumonia's the danger.'

Fiona said, 'Langley's blaming himself for not being there.'

'Is he?' said George. 'If the worst happens he'll get around to blaming Sian or Barney.'

Sian's room was full of moonlight, and she didn't turn on the light. The shape of the rocking horse glimmered pearly white, and she went across and stroked his mane. She thought, I wish you did grow wings after midnight, I'd like to fly away tonight.

There was a small aching lump in her throat for Emily, and she didn't expect to get much sleep herself. She was still wearing Phyllis Barker's clothes. She wondered where she had set down Mrs. Barker's jar of chutney, and she couldn't remember. She stripped off the jumper and skirt in the darkness, and prayed for Emily and for Langley, and felt that she would have bartered ten years of life to have looked in to say good-bye to Emily before she went off with Barney.

She slept, in snatches. Each time she woke she remembered and the darkness seemed a little darker. She came downstairs early; she wanted to get across to the gallery. She'd cook breakfast, they had to eat something, and she wanted to be with Langley when they got the first news of the day.

It was about half-past seven, and as she reached the top of the staircase from her floor she looked down on George, replacing the telephone. He was still in dressing gown. She asked, 'Was that the hospital?'

'Yes, I called them.' Fiona had probably asked him to ring as soon as she awoke. He said, 'They say she's comfortable.'

'They always say that, don't they?'

'And she had a good night.'

'She was drugged.'

'Yes.'

As Sian hurried downstairs Fiona came out of the bedroom, and Sian heard George telling her, 'She's comfortable, she's had a good night . . .' that glib little medical placebo that meant nothing.

She passed two neighbours in the street who asked, 'Any news?' and she said,

'She's had a good night,' and they said,

'I am glad.'

She let herself into the gallery, it was too early for the mail, there were no letters on the mat. She hoped Langley wasn't up. If he was in bed he had to be resting, even if he wasn't sleeping.

All the doors into the hall were closed, there was no sound or sign of life until she opened the kitchen door and saw Phyllis.

Sian stared. She didn't say, 'What are you doing here?' because she could see that Phyllis was laying the table. Instead she asked, 'Have you been here all night?'

Sian and Fiona had left Phyllis about half-past ten last night, showing every sign of getting into her car and driving herself home. But she was here at half-past seven this morning, so it was possible she had changed her plans.

Phyllis said, 'I came about half an hour ago.'

'Why?'

To look in and offer help was neighbourly. To move in and look so much at home was suspect, on the part of a girl admittedly infatuated with Langley.

'Barney asked me to,' said Phyllis. 'Last night.' She was uncertain of her welcome here, as well she might be. 'Just while Emily's away, of course. Someone's got to cook, and look after the house, and things like that.'

It was hard to get domestic help. Even in a village whose only industry was the shops in the high street and the farms around, the women who wanted jobs were either serving in the shops or finding employment in the nearest town; and it would have been almost impossible to secure a housekeeper.

But they could have found someone to lend a hand with the housework say two days a week, and Sian would have set to herself, and managed the cooking. She did not want

Phyllis Barker here. Anyone but Phyllis.

Langley might smile and call Phyllis a child, but Phyllis was exactly six months younger than Sian herself. She was a woman, and she could cause a lot of trouble, and she was almost certainly going to get hurt.

Barney couldn't have stopped to consider a thing, except the inconvenience of a part-time housekeeper instead of a full-time one.

Sian said, tight-lipped, 'Does Langley know about this?'

'I think so, yes. Barney asked me as I was getting into my car to go home, I think he went back and told Langley.'

'Have you seen either of them this morning?'

'Not Langley, no. Barney let me in.' She looked so woe-begone that Sian felt a bully. You couldn't blame Phyllis. Barney was the one who should have had sense enough to see that making Phyllis part of this household was putting a fuse to a highly explosive situation. 'Then he went out,' said Phyllis plaintively.

'When he comes back,' said Sian, with determination, 'I'll have a few words with him.'

Phyllis got on with the breakfast, and Sian – with nothing to do in the kitchen, Phyllis was managing beautifully – went into the studio and did a little more work on the minia-ture. She found her jar of chutney on a table by the door. She must have put it there when Barney called last night, before she ran to see Emily. She worked doggedly, trying to keep her mind on her painting, jumping up when the door bell rang and cornering Barney in the display room. She asked, 'You've been through to the hospital?'

'Yes, she's had a quiet night.'

'George rang, that's what they told him.'

She stepped into Barney's path to check him for a mo-ment, this had to be discussed before they went into the house. 'Now about Phyllis Barker, it isn't fair to let her start working here.'

'Not fair on who?'

'On Phyllis, of course. You know how she feels about Langley.'

'What do you think she's going to do – seduce him?'

He sounded weary – perhaps he hadn't slept so well either – and Sian said tartly, 'Don't be so sickeningly cool! I don't think anything of the sort, but from what I've heard and seen she's capable of making a blessed nuisance of herself, and Langley's got enough worries right now.'

'She's also – although I don't suppose this worries you one way or the other – capable of being hurt. So why do it? Why tell her to move in? I'll see to your meals, and you can surely to goodness make your own bed.'

'You've got no time to see to anybody's meals,' said Barney. 'You've got two jobs going already.'

'Joss Ennerman can forget the modelling.'

'He won't, you know. He's decided you have talent and you're not treating it right, and he'll be back if he doesn't hear from you soon. He's a forceful chap, very capable of telling Langley to get out of the way.'

Langley wouldn't like that, and neither would Sian.

She said, 'I could manage. The neighbours would help.'

'A neighbour is helping,' he pointed out. 'Phyllis. And she's the only one with time to kill. Of course if you can't trust Langley with her—'

She scowled, 'Of course I can.'

'Right, then. As for her being hurt, she's more likely to be painlessly cured of her crush on Langley by the time she's cooked and cleaned for him for a few weeks.' He went past Sian, asking, 'How did you sleep?'

'Not too badly.' It seemed that discussion was over, and Phyllis was staying, but Sian still wasn't happy about it. She would talk to Langley. Langley was the unselfish one, he wouldn't want anybody to risk being hurt.

Langley was in the kitchen. He had just come down and Phyllis was hovering around like a mother hen, trying to get him to peck at his breakfast. He hadn't slept, the shadows were dark under his eyes, and Sian went to him, asking again, 'Have you been through to the hospital?'

'Of course. I rang about seven o'clock.' Of course he had.

'They said she was comfortable, but they always say that, don't they?'

Maybe they did, but now she argued, 'It must mean she's holding her own. If they were scared of pneumonia it must mean there's no sign of that yet, mustn't it?'

Phyllis put a plate of bacon and eggs in front of Langley and he pushed it away. Sian said, 'Do eat something.'

'Sorry,' said Langley, 'I'm just not hungry.'

'Who is?' said Barney. 'But starving ourselves isn't going to help Emily.' He poured out coffee and took toast, and Langley said,

'Coffee, then. Sorry, but I can't eat.'

They all drank coffee. It was strange to see Phyllis sitting there in Emily's chair. No one said much, there wasn't much to say. The phone rang a couple of times. Each time Barney answered it while the others sat still and stony-faced, but it was only neighbours wanting a bulletin.

Barney got up first, and Langley asked, 'Where are you going?'

'Over to the stores.'

'To work?' It passed Langley's comprehension, it passed Sian's too. 'You can sit and write fiction when Emily could be dying?'

'What else is there to do?'

'You could come to the hospital with me.' Langley looked steadily at Barney. 'If it's necessary I suppose I can ring you on George's number?'

'Yes.'

'Try to get there in time this time, will you?' Langley was angry. His voice was contemptuous, and there was a bitter whiteness around his mouth.

Barney frowned slightly, and Sian saw a muscle leap in his cheek. Then he said 'I will,' and went, and they heard the doors closing behind him.

Phyllis's eyes were wide on Langley, and Sian could think of nothing to say or do, and Langley said, 'Sorry' to both of them, apologizing for the little scene and their embarrassment. He said bleakly, 'I envy my brother. He's always been able to switch off, opt out. It's a gift, isn't it? It makes life much easier for him.' He sighed and looked at Sian, making himself businesslike with an effort. 'Now, can you cope with the gallery today?'

'Yes, of course.'

'Good. I must be at the hospital, you understand?'

She understood. 'If you'd just glance through any mail there is, first—'

'Yes,' said Langley.

They went into the studio and she collected the mail. There was nothing she couldn't deal with, and she said, 'Give Emily my love. Tell her we miss her very much.'

'She may never come back. You do realize that?'

'She will,' said Sian stubbornly. 'Oh, before you go there's one other thing – Phyllis.'

'What about Phyllis?'

'I don't think Barney should have asked her to come and housekeep for you. She still has a crush on you and there could be a lot of complications.'

He thought she was making difficulties. He said patiently, 'You exaggerate. She's a nice girl, there'll be no complications.' What had being a nice girl got to do with it? Sian smiled at his naïveté, but his next argument was valid. 'We've got to have somebody to run the house, you can't do it, you've got enough right here. We're lucky to get Phyllis.'

'I still think—'

He was wearying, although his voice stayed gentle. 'If you can find someone else do, but don't bother me with it at the moment, please. Do you mind?'

She mustn't nag now, not now. Perhaps she could find someone else, and maybe she was making mountains. As Barney said – couldn't she trust Langley? And Phyllis must know the risk she was taking. If she got hurt it was a pity, but there didn't seem to be much Sian could do about it.

'All right,' she said. 'You'll phone me? You'll let me know how Emily is?'

'Yes, I will.' He took her hands between his. 'You care, don't you? You'll be waiting for the phone call. If I ring Barney how long do you think it will take him to get back to real life, and realize it's Emily we're talking about?'

She couldn't answer that. She kissed him instead, and he held her close, as though her warmth was his defence against Barney's detachment, before he went.

It was a busy day. Working on her own it was bound to be, and then there were all the people who looked in to ask after Emily. Just as they had looked in to ask about Barney after the car crash. 'Two accidents,' said one old soul with relish. 'Bound to be a third.'

'Nonsense!' Sian snapped, edgy enough without this sort of Job's comfort. That first day everyone was gloomy. Emily's accident was bad enough, but the idea of her lying there calling for help was added horror, and they dwelt on it – nobody's fault, of course, but just imagine. Sian so near and not hearing and not knowing – until Sian wasn't sure whether she was going to sob or scream, but was convinced that one or the other was about to happen.

She got through the day, and so did Emily. Emily proved resilient. She didn't get pneumonia, although the kind of fracture she had was enough complication in itself. After three days they knew it wasn't going to kill her, but she would never again run upstairs or climb on another chair. Whether she would ever walk was still a matter of conjecture.

Sian suffered with Langley. His sensitive mind was still torturing him, so that he found it hard to accept medical assurance that the danger was past. He was afraid of relapse, and each time he saw Emily he came out full of forebodings.

Sian was badly shaken the first time they let her go in to visit Emily. She looked shrivelled up, as though she had suddenly grown much older than her years. Before she had looked younger, she was sixty-eight; now she could have passed for ninety.

The white coverlet of her bed was raised, and she was

propped up, her once-ruddy cheeks the colour of coverlet and pillow. This was a short visit, confined to a few whispered words and a squeeze of the hands. Sian wept, outside in the car, and Langley sat haggard over the wheel, saying again and again, 'Why wasn't I there? Why didn't you go in? Why? Why?'

The next visit was better. A week after the accident Emily was out of bed, sitting in a wheelchair, when they arrived. She couldn't walk, but her face was plumper, the shrivelled skin smoother, and Sian said, 'Hey, you look wonderful!' She did not, but she certainly looked better.

'So they keep telling me,' said Emily. 'Never mind about my beauty, how long's it going to be before I get out of here?'

'You've got to learn to walk again,' the nurse sounded as though this was a small treat in store. 'You do what you're told and be a good girl, and you'll be skipping around in no time at all.'

Emily looked at her with scorn, but no one told Emily that the latest reports were that she was going to be in the nursing home about three months, and that was a conservative estimate.

Most of Emily's steady stream of visitors had told her that Phyllis Barker was looking after Barney and Langley. She waited to ask Sian, 'What's Phyllis Barker doing?' She had already asked Barney and Langley, and they had told her that Phyllis was doing fine. Cooking adequately and keeping down the dust. Not like Emily, of course, but holding the fort till Emily's return.

It was still Sian's reaction that Emily wanted, and when Sian said fine too, Emily said, 'Well, I hope she's got more sense than she used to have.' Langley had smiled, and Emily had said, darkly, 'Never mind . . .'

Phyllis still couldn't believe her luck. She was lucky she felt for the first time in her life, being here, seeing Langley every day. When Barney had said, 'Phyllis, you don't know anyone who'd come in and keep the place ticking over, do you?' she had heard herself say,

'I would. I'd like to.' But she hadn't believed it.

She had gone home. And she was round at the Little Gallery at seven o'clock next morning, with her finger on the doorbell.

By the end of the week Sian was accepting her. There hadn't been time to look for a replacement, because Langley wasn't home all that much that first week, and perversely there had been a brisk flow of customers. Sian was busy. She did some work on her modelling, mostly late at night, and whether it was any good or not she found it an escape from the stress and strain of the days following Emily's accident.

Like Langley she envied Barney's gift for switching off. He could submerge everything in his work, going over to the stores every morning. He did visit Emily, he did talk about her, he did seem to care. To his way of thinking he probably had things in proportion. But Sian couldn't divide life into watertight compartments. She was like Langley. She stayed worried about Emily all the time.

And then Natalie Wender came down . . .

CHAPTER EIGHT

SIAN was visiting Emily today. It was just over a fortnight now since the accident, and Emily was doing her daily exercises; but she was still unable to stand, let alone walk. She fretted at her own inaction, and worried how Barney and Langley were managing without her.

Phyllis had been into the nursing home, earlier in the week, and come out with instructions on the kind of food Langley liked, and the order in which the rooms should be cleaned. Phyllis was anxious to please, and Emily conceded that there was less silliness in her than you'd think. At least she was ready to take advice, and she had promised to call once a week and consult Emily about the menus.

Sian gave Emily all the news she had, and messages from some of the neighbours, and told her what they'd sold in the gallery today and yesterday, and that Fiona and George were planning to redecorate their living-room and couldn't agree on the ceiling colour.

Barney was supposed to be coming this afternoon, said Emily, and he was late. While she was listening to Sian her eyes kept darting to the door, and Sian's chatter only had half her attention.

She was out of bed, in an armchair by the window. 'It's a pretty view,' Sian said desperately.

Trees, lawns criss-crossed with paved paths down which the patients might walk or be wheeled, but not on damp dull days like today. Sian thought, if Barney doesn't come I'll break up his concentration when I get back. Work's probably going well, and Emily's a poor second, but he won't shut out what I'll have to say to him if I have to shout it through a megaphone.

Langley came every day, leaving Sian in charge of the gallery. But today he had stayed behind and Sian had come, and Barney had promised, and Barney wasn't here.

Then there was a flurry in the doorway and Natalie Wender swooped in, making little cooing noises, her arms so full of red roses it was a wonder she could see where she was going. Barney was just behind her, and Emily beamed, reaching out her hands for Natalie and Barney and the roses.

'Surprise, surprise!' sang Natalie. She dumped the roses on a table and some spilled over on to the floor, and it was either the roses or Natalie, but the air was full of perfume. The skies through the window were still dull, but in here it was golden.

Sitting on the hard-backed chair by the window Sian thought, you're a surprise all right. I thought I remembered what a knock-out you are, but I didn't. One look at you and Barney would decide to opt for real life today. You wouldn't need a megaphone to get through to him. All you'd have to do is stand there.

'It was a surprise to me too,' said Barney. He kissed Emily's cheek. 'Sorry we're late, Emmy, but it's worth it, isn't it?'

Natalie was in a cream silk trouser suit and flat golden sandals. She shimmered. All the light in the room seemed to have settled around her, on the smooth sheen of her cheekbones, touching the gleams in her hair. She said, 'I was told I wouldn't be needed till Tuesday,' today was Saturday, 'so I tossed in a toothbrush and came. I rang Barney when I was about ten miles away.' She smiled at him. 'And he waited for me, and we came straight out to see you.'

She kissed Emily's cheek, too, bending over her. 'Poor Emily, how are you?' Her compassion was as warm and soft as the scent of the roses. 'You've had a horrid time, haven't you?'

'It wasn't so good,' Emily admitted.

'Never mind,' Natalie patted Emily's hand. 'You have a nice rest while you can. Don't you be in too much of a hurry to get back. They'll appreciate you all the more for being without you for a bit.'

She smiled again at Barney, a quick flirt of those incredible eyelashes, and he grinned back and Sian could have said, 'I told you so. I told you you wouldn't lose her.'

'Hello,' Natalie said to Sian.

'Hello,' Sian echoed.

A nurse put her head round the door and gasped at the flood of crimson roses, 'My goodness, it's like a garden! I don't know whether we've got enough vases.'

Emily laughed at being spoiled so extravagantly, and enjoyed sending most of the roses to other patients in other rooms and wards, keeping one gorgeous bowlful for herself.

Sian didn't have to rack her mind over what else she could say to interest Emily, because they had Natalie now, and Natalie had a bubbling flow of anecdotes. Mostly about the film she was making. She talked about all the hitches and the funny moments until she had Emily weak with laughter. She never stopped talking. When she was through with the film she moved on to people, describing them for Emily and Sian so that she wasn't boring for a moment.

Emily was really enjoying herself, and so was Sian, of course. Natalie was a born entertainer, the world she was talking about was tight-packed with incident, and Barney must be feeling more nostalgic for it by the minute. No wonder he resented being stuck down here.

When the little bell rang and it was time for visitors to leave Emily said, '*Never!* You don't seem to have been here more than five minutes.'

Sian wouldn't have said that. It seemed to her that she had been listening to Natalie for a long time.

Natalie's little red sports car was outside in the car park, and Barney said, 'How are you getting back?' to Sian.

'I came on the bus.'

She went back with Barney and Natalie, sitting beside Natalie, while Barney sat with his long legs jammed somehow into what was very much an emergency rear seat. He climbed out with relief at the other end and uncoiled. 'Strictly for pygmies,' he said.

Natalie shrugged and laughed. She hadn't invited Sian to

travel with them, Barney had.

Sian said, 'Thanks, anyhow.'

'You're welcome,' said Barney. 'I feel like a trussed chicken.'

He and Natalie got back in the car, and Sian went into the gallery. It was still open, but the blind in the studio was drawn, and as she reached an instinctive hand for the light switch Langley said sharply, 'Don't!'

'What's the matter?'

'I've got a migraine coming on.'

She went across to where he sat. He was pale, his forehead dabbled with sweat. Sian didn't get migraines, but Aunt Mary had had them, and she knew that Langley did. She asked, 'Have you taken something?' and he said,

'I'm rattling with pills.'

'You should have closed the gallery and gone to bed.'

That was the only effective treatment. Drugs might deaden the pain, but Langley was going to be fit for nothing for the next few hours. Bed was the place for him. She urged, 'Go along, darling. It's nearly five o'clock anyway.'

'You're sure?' He swayed as he stood, and she turned him towards the door, with a supporting hand.

'Go along,' she said again.

'How was Emily?'

'Fine, especially after Barney and Natalie Wender arrived. You know Natalie's here?'

'Yes.' He smiled weakly. 'That would brighten her up. Any sign of her getting on her feet yet?'

'I spoke to the matron on my way in. They're satisfied. Progress is bound to be slow.'

Langley nodded and flinched, and she went with him to the bottom of the stairs. She wished he would stop worrying about Emily. That was what caused the headaches, and a flare-up of that back condition. When he was overtired, overworried, that old riding injury always plagued him.

Phyllis came out of the kitchen, to catch a final glimpse of Langley at the top of the stairs, and Sian said, 'He's going to lie down. He's got a migraine.'

Since Emily's accident Langley had had more than one headache. Emily's accident had been one long headache, physical for Langley as well as emotional, and it was not at all surprising that they were culminating in a raging migraine.

Phyllis asked, 'Has he taken anything for it?'

'I asked him. Yes, he has.'

Phyllis strained to watch the slow-moving figure go. Her voice was anguished. 'My mother has migraines. She says they're next door to dying.' She sounded as though the black death had struck, and Sian said with deliberate cheerfulness,

'They haven't killed your mother and they won't kill Langley.' She wasn't unfeeling, she was very sorry for Langley, but wringing their hands in chorus at the bottom of the stairs wasn't going to help. So she went back into the gallery to wait around for the next half hour in case any customers came. None did, and she closed on time. She and Langley should have been going out tonight, nowhere very exciting, to the cinema, but she had looked forward to it, and now of course it was out of the question.

She went up to Langley's room, and opened the door quietly. He was lying, his face turned away from the door, and he didn't move. She hoped he was asleep, and not on that plane of pain where movement can plunge thin white daggers through the brain. She crept over and put a note on the bedside table, then crept out again and closed the door carefully so that it made only the faintest click.

Phyllis was in the drawing room, with a duster in her hands. 'How is he?' she wanted to know.

'Asleep,' said Sian.

'That's good,' said Phyllis, on a long sigh of relief as though she had been holding her breath. 'He'll be better when he wakes up.' She added, 'I've fixed the room for Miss Wender.' She sighed again, this time in wonder. 'Isn't she fantastic? I think she's the loveliest girl I've ever seen.'

'Yes,' said Sian. She went, feeling depressed; Langley's migraine, the lonely evening ahead, Natalie Wender's breathtaking, riveting beauty, somehow combining to leave a taste like ashes in her mouth.

She prepared her tea in Fiona's kitchen: a pot of tea, a slice of cake, and two rounds of toast. Fiona looked in as she was buttering the toast. There were still ten minutes to go before the stores closed, but by now on a Saturday evening you were only getting the occasional late shopper. Fiona was killing time, waiting for six o'clock.

'Hello,' said Fiona. 'I hear Barney's girl-friend's back again.'

'Yes. She brought about five hundred roses to the nursing home for Emily this afternoon.'

Fiona looked impressed, 'That was quite a gesture. What did you take?'

'A bunch of grapes and a box of shortbread,' said Sian. 'They vanished under the roses.'

Fiona stood in the doorway, watching the stairs. 'Never mind, they'll turn up again. Shortbread lasts longer than roses. Going out tonight?'

'No, Langley has a migraine.'

Fiona winced in sympathy, she suffered from the odd sick headache herself. 'I'm not surprised, he's been under a lot of strain lately. Come down and watch television and put your feet up with us.'

'Thank you,' said Sian. 'I might very well do that.'

She poured Fiona a cup of tea, and carried her tray upstairs to her own room; and as Fiona lifted the cup to her lips three customers came up from the ground floor.

Sian ate her tea slowly. If the bus service had been a scrap more reliable she would have gone into town alone and seen that film. She could work on her model, but she didn't want to. She would end no doubt in going downstairs, because she enjoyed being with George and Fiona, but it was only fair to give them time to have a meal and unwind first. Saturday was the busiest day in the week up to the last half hour. It would be about seven o'clock before company should be inflicted on them. Any company.

So Sian ate her tea, and washed and changed, although

her day's get-up of the pink shirt-dress would have done well enough for an evening watching television with George and Fiona. She put on the harebell angora instead. She had bought that for her first date with Langley, the one that Barney had spoiled.

Tonight poor Langley was blinded with migraine, and Barney was taking Natalie to the Royal. Natalie had said, as they drove back from Ivy House, 'Where shall we eat tonight?' and Barney had said,

'The Royal isn't bad.'

When he walked in with Natalie every man in the room would envy him, and every woman would have to try a little harder. When he had walked in with Sian the other diners probably noticed Barney – with an arm in a sling and that scar across his face who wouldn't? – but nobody had looked twice at Sian.

Before she settled for her evening with the McDades she would pop back to the gallery, check again on Langley's progress. She had left a note beside him, asking him to ring her if he had a miracle recovery but knowing he wouldn't. She hoped Barney and Natalie would have gone, there was no denying that Natalie Wender in the same room made Sian feel not only plain by comparison but stupid too, as though nothing she could say would hold anyone's attention for a moment.

She let herself into the gallery, and walked through into the house. She could hear a radio playing softly in the kitchen and went towards it. Phyllis was supposed to go home at six o'clock, but she was still here finishing the ironing, backed by a pile of crisp shirts.

Sian said, 'I thought they were non-iron,' and Phyllis looked at her handiwork,

'They are, but they come up better if you iron them.'

'It seems a waste of time to me,' said Sian, smiling.

'Does it?' Phyllis smoothed down a cuff. 'I suppose it is,' she said in a small voice, 'but I like ironing.'

'There's no better reason for doing it,' said Sian. 'Has everyone gone?'

'Barney and Miss Wender? Yes. And Langley's still asleep, I peeped in a few minutes ago.'

So Sian could go back and watch television with George and Fiona. There was nothing to do here; Phyllis was on the last shirt, Langley was sleeping. A few cups, saucers and plates stood on the draining board, dry now, and Sian took them over to the Welsh dresser.

Phyllis was still reeling under the impact of Natalie Wender. She said, 'I saw Miss Wender on the television, but I still can't get over the way she looks. And she's so friendly, isn't she? She came and talked to me, asked me all about myself. She's making a film, isn't she?'

Sian nodded, hanging a cup on its hook with care. 'We'll have to go and see it,' said Phyllis. She took the shirt off the ironing board and gave it a little shake before folding. 'I should have thought Barney would have had a picture of her in his room, shouldn't you?'

'Maybe he doesn't need one,' said Sian. 'I doubt if any man would forget what she looks like.'

Phyllis, conscious of being completely forgettable, drooped a little as she put this shirt with the others. She said, 'Do you think I ought to look in again on Langley before I go? Make sure there's nothing he needs.'

'I will,' said Sian.

This time Langley opened his eyes as she stood beside the bed, and she asked gently, 'How is it?'

'Pretty grim,' he said.

'You don't want anything?'

'No. Just rest.'

She came out of the room, and waited while Phyllis put on her hat and coat, and the two girls left the gallery together. Left behind Phyllis was capable of peering in on the invalid at five-minute intervals, killing by kindness.

Sian spent the evening with Fiona and George. It was a pleasant, restful evening; George slept for some of it, head back in his armchair, while Fiona and Sian watched the television and gossiped about nothing in particular, and cooked sausages for supper.

She went back to her own room just before midnight, and pottered around, ready for bed but with no urgency because tomorrow was Sunday morning and she could sleep late. She read a while, a thriller someone had recommended, and tried out a few hairstyles from a magazine. Then she got into bed, and lay relaxed and waiting for sleep.

She hoped Langley was feeling better. She wondered if Barney and Natalie were home yet. After midnight there wasn't much to do round here. Even in town the restaurants closed and the one and only discotheque was hardly up to Barney Hollis and Natalie Wender standards.

She squirmed impatiently, trying to get them out of her mind, and sat up and pummelled her pillow, then lay down again and listened to the wind sobbing and tapping against the old window frames. It was a lonely sound. In her warm bed in the warm room it brought a coldness where she felt that her heart should be . . .

Next morning Langley was up, but not about. Sian rang through just after breakfast, and he told her he felt better but today he was taking things easy.

'Of course,' she said. 'And you can, it's Sunday. I'll be over later. I thought I might do some reorganizing in the display room.'

She had Sunday lunch as usual with Fiona and George, and went over to the gallery mid-afternoon. Barney and Natalie had gone out for the day, and Phyllis had left just before Sian got there. Phyllis cooked a midday meal on Sundays, and Sunday was her half-day. She had offered to stay on, but Langley had said there was no need at all. He said he was better, but he was looking and undoubtedly feeling jaded, and when Sian suggested he stayed in the drawing-room, resting, while she got on with her display room changes he raised no objections.

She moved in some new pieces, recently acquired, and shifted others around. She liked to feel that the gallery wasn't getting into a rut, that it was a place that customers would return to as often as they could because there was always the chance of them finding something they liked today, even if they hadn't last week. She dusted and polished, and set up a small exhibition of near-antique writing equipment: ornate inkwells, silver-handled ivory paper knives, paperweights. Then she got tea for herself and Langley, and they played some records and talked desultorily because Langley's headache was still with him.

'I do feel,' said Sian, 'that an early night's on the cards for you. And if you don't feel fit in the morning I can cope.'

'I know you can,' said Langley. 'I'm so lucky to have found you.' He looked fine-drawn with fatigue, and regretful. 'I'd thought we might have gone to Deniston Crag today.'

. . . 'Next time you ask me, perhaps,' she'd said. 'We'll go to Deniston Crag again . . .'

Now Langley said, 'I suppose it wouldn't do if I asked you here? If I said now – Sian, will you marry me?'

She had been kneeling in front of the record player, taking off records, and she got up because there was a greyish pallor beneath the tan of Langley's skin. She said, 'You're going back to bed, and if you're no better in the morning I'm getting the doctor round.'

'I don't need a doctor. These migraines usually hang on for two or three days.'

'You shouldn't have got up today.'

He said wearily, 'You may be right.'

Next morning she insisted on him keeping out of the gallery and in the house. The migraine had been a bad one. It had left him drained of energy, and he had a day's convalescence because on Tuesday there was a sale to attend, with a prospect of cut-throat bidding, and he was going to need a clear head.

Sian hadn't seen Barney or Natalie at all on Sunday, and she went home Monday evening without having seen either of them that day. Natalie was leaving Monday night – she started filming again in the morning – and Sian was startled when she went to answer a tap on the door and there stood Natalie.

Natalie smiled radiantly. 'I just came over to say good-bye. He said to come up.' George must have let her in. Sian was so taken aback that she was dumbstruck. Natalie Wender had a pervading charm, but she hadn't used it before on Sian, and Sian would never have expected her to take this trouble.

She said, 'How nice of you. Do come in for a minute. Is Barney with you?'

'No, he was on the phone, so I took my chance.' Natalie saw the rocking horse at once and went across to it, making the little cooing noises she had made at Emily. 'The pet! Isn't he beautiful? Yes, I remember him. So he ended up with you.'

Sian was glad Natalie didn't know how near she had been to getting the rocking horse herself. She would have liked it. She said, 'You're not open to offers, I suppose?'

'Sorry.'

'I don't blame you. I wouldn't part with him either. I asked Barney about him, but he said he'd gone.'

In the silence, while Natalie looked at the rocking horse, Sian asked the obvious, 'Have you had a nice week-end?'

'Lovely! I'm sorry to be going back.'

Sorry to be leaving Barney, she meant, but if the week-end had been that lovely there would be enough memories to bridge the waiting till they were together again.

Natalie said, 'While I'm saying good-bye I'd like to give you some advice, I hope you won't be offended.' She stood still, her huge eyes on Sian.

'What advice?'

'Phyllis Barker! If I were you, sweetie, I'd get her out fast.'

'Why?'

'You fancy Langley, don't you? Well, so does she. I've been watching her, and she's not so bright, but she does have the knack of making herself indispensable about the house. I like Langley,' said Natalie, 'and frankly I like you too. I think you're right for each other, but you could have trouble on your hands with little Miss Barker.'

That was so exactly Sian's own fear, although she had

pushed it away. She said, 'Phyllis has had a crush on Langley for years. She's the last girl I should have chosen to take over as housekeeper.'

'Then why did you choose her?' Natalie was amazed. 'Didn't you have *any* say in it?'

'Not much. Barney engaged her. It isn't easy to get help about the house, and Phyllis was there the night Emily was hurt.'

'*Barney?*' Natalie said the name slowly, as though it was the key, making everything plain as day. She began to laugh. 'Barney, was it? And he of course knew that little Phyllis carries a torch for brother Langley?'

'Yes, but I don't suppose he stopped to think—'

'Barney always stops to think,' said Natalie. 'You kid yourself he's acting all impulsive, then you realize it's only because his brain works time-and-a-half faster than average.'

Natalie might know what she was talking about, but Sian didn't. Natalie explained, 'Barney likes things moving. The quiet life kills him. If there isn't a happening to hand he'll start one.'

Things happened around Barney Hollis, everybody noticed that.

'So he takes on Phyllis Barker as housekeeper,' Natalie elaborated, 'and I'll bet he's got it all down in notes, just waiting for the big scene. He's an obsessive writer, it's all grist to the mill.'

'I can't believe that.'

'I can.' Natalie was positive. 'And nobody knows him better than I do. Anyhow, you take my advice, sweetie, you give her her marching orders.'

Sian was disarmed by Natalie's concern. She said, 'Thank you,' although she still didn't know what to believe. She said, much too brightly, 'You wouldn't like to stay here and keep an eye on Barney, would you? You might keep him out of mischief.'

Natalie put her head on one side, screwing her face into a gay grimace. 'I'd need notice of that. He'd have to do more than crook a finger to keep me down here, he'd have to really beg.' For a moment her face shadowed, and her voice. 'And Barney will never want anything enough to beg for it.' She smiled again. 'Still—' she said, and hugged herself, then laughed at what she was thinking, said good-bye to Sian, and hurried back to the gallery where the little red car was parked and ready to go.

'I went to get some cigarettes,' she told Barney.

Sian sat down on the divan and looped her hands round her knees. 'And who would have expected that?' she asked the rocking horse, 'such thoughtfulness on the part of Natalie Wender! Although how I'm going to get Phyllis out I would not know.' She sat quiet for a while. 'Maybe,' she said, 'Barney would like to write the script for me.'

That was a chilling little thought, Barney waiting for the emotional blast-off when everybody was going to start shouting or sobbing or rushing out into the night. Natalie had said, 'I'll bet he's got it all down in his notes.' That meant he must keep files about the people he met, right from the beginning, jotting down conversations, tricks of expression and gesture. 'For inspiration you can't beat the human race,' that was Barney. Open any door, look behind the eyes, and there's your jungle . . .

She went to the curtain dividing the rooms and pulled it aside. He kept a tidy desk: top on the tape recorder, the typewriter covered, unused paper stacked in a neatish pile. The table had two drawers, wide enough for files.

She had no idea how the tape-recorder worked, she had never used one, but she stood on a packing case now and plugged it into the light socket. The on-off switch was self-explanatory, but she shrank from the risk of snarling up all that tape by taking a chance with the other controls. Instead she sat down and opened a drawer: more typing paper, a couple of ribbons, carbons. The second drawer was full of large brown paper envelopes, fairly bulky, and she was easing out the top one when Barney said, 'If you'll tell me what you're looking for I'll tell you if you're likely to find it.'

She hadn't heard him come up the stairs. He stood in the doorway, then wended his way between the boxes and the racks towards the dais.

She stayed where she was, sitting, her fingertips on the edge of the open drawer. Chin up to emphasize that she wasn't cringing, she wasn't ashamed of being caught going through his papers, and when he was the other side of the table she threw in the challenge, 'I've just had a talk with Natalie.'

'Have you?'

'It was interesting. Natalie says you brought Phyllis Barker in while Emily was away because you like to keep things moving. Because you're an obsessive writer and everything is grist to the mill.'

'True.' He sounded as though they were playing a parlour game. 'Up to a point.'

She was stiff with disapproval. 'That's your line and your business. But I would like to know exactly what you're jotting down about us all.'

'Would you?' He came round the desk and shut the drawer, smartly enough for her to have to snatch her fingers away.

She still couldn't believe it. '*Did* you ask Phyllis Barker to work for Langley mainly because you know how she feels about him?'

'Yes.'

'That was a fairly monstrous thing. What are you hoping for, suicide or murder?'

'Sorry to disappoint you.' He sounded sorry. 'Neither. It was a simple brotherly act, entirely for Langley's well-being. Phyllis is willing to devote her life to Langley and love every minute of it. She's going to make him an excellent wife.'

Sian got up then. She scrambled to her feet so that she knocked back the chair. This had to be a joke in doubtful taste, but she had the strangest feeling that it wasn't. 'You're not fooling, are you?'

He shook his head.

'Then you must be out of your mind if you think Langley's going to jilt me for Phyllis!'

How dared he interfere like this? Phyllis might have the makings of a good wife, a good housewife anyway, but Langley loved Sian and it was in no way any concern of Barney's, and how *dared* he? She said, as though the words came through chipped ice, 'I have news for you. Langley asked me to marry him this afternoon.'

'And what did you say?'

'What do you think I said?'

One eyebrow shot up sceptically. 'I think you put it off. I think you're fooling yourself. When it comes to the crunch of truth you don't want to marry Langley.'

She hadn't put it off. Langley had looked ill, been ill. And the time before – there had been reasons then why she hadn't said, 'Yes.' Not because she didn't want to marry Langley, just reasons why she didn't say, 'Yes' at that particular time.

It was disconcerting that Barney guessed she hadn't committed herself, but she was certainly not discussing it with him. She stepped off the dais to get round to her own room. 'Natalie was right,' he said. He picked up the chair and put a foot on it, right arm slung across his knee in the stance of a casual lecturer. 'I do watch people, I do try to find out what makes them tick. When I first met you I thought you were a Phyllis Barker, with the added bonus of a sense of humour and a fairly good business head.'

She walked towards the archway. 'Since then,' he went on, 'I've realized I was wrong. You're too talented and too tough for Langley. In twelve months' time you'll have a name as a promising young sculptor and you'll go on from there. You're not the right girl for Langley, you'd be no wife for him at all.'

She turned, as she swished the curtain aside, to look back at him with dislike. 'I didn't ask to be turned into a career girl. You started that, bringing Joss Ennerman into it, but I can stop it any time I like.'

She didn't want to be an artist, she just wanted Langley and a quiet life of loving and giving. She went across to the head and took off the wet cloth, and behind her Barney said, 'All right, smash it, you'll make another.'

To destroy it now would be a childish gesture. She covered it again. She said, 'If I should turn up in one of your scripts, no matter how heavily disguised, I shall sue like crazy.'

'I'll remember.'

'And get a key for that drawer if you need to keep your files to yourself.'

'I've got a key.' He stood, looking at her, eyes narrowed and intent, and she wondered if he was seeing this little scene as possible 'copy'. It made her flesh crawl. She said, 'Go away, will you?'

'You know what Langley is to you?'

'Yes. And I don't need you to tell me.'

'He's Aunt Mary's heir and successor. You had your life so full caring for her that when she died you were left with a void, and no idea at the time how to fill it.'

She clenched her teeth so hard that her jaw ached a little. 'You were never in love with Langley,' said Barney. 'You were just missing Aunt Mary.'

'I love Langley.' If you can shriek quietly she did it. 'Not your kind of loving either.'

'And what do you know about my kind of loving?'

'What Langley's told me about you. And Natalie.'

'Let's take Natalie.'

'She said you'd never need anyone enough to beg.'

'Right again.'

His words seemed to be coming slower as hers came faster. 'I'm sure she is. But you're not. You're wrong about everything.' He shrugged. She said furiously, 'Don't worry about Langley. Nor about me.'

'I'm not worried about you. The world may well be your oyster.'

She must stop this. Bickering with Barney about Langley was less than undignified, it was insane. 'My patience is getting very thin,' she said. 'Why don't you go right away?' and he grinned suddenly,

'Any day now, love. Don't forget to let me know about the wedding.'

'And what guarantee have I that you wouldn't jump up and try to stop it?'

'Why should I? He'll be marrying Phyllis.'

She didn't know whether to laugh or cry after that lot. A more impossible man never breathed. As Natalie Wender who knew him best had said, a natural stirrer, anything to break the monotony. Well, this was a pretty poor joke, because now Phyllis would have to go. She constituted no real rivalry, Sian knew that, but the longer she stayed the harder it was going to be for her.

If they couldn't get a housekeeper the dust would have to lie. Sian could manage meals, she'd clean up in the evenings and they'd just have to advertise and hope.

She wasn't looking forward to sacking Phyllis. She was angry with Barney for having put her in this position, and a little of her resentment extended to Langley, because he could have stopped it before it started. That first morning would have been the time.

She watched Phyllis at breakfast with an impersonal eye, seeing, as Natalie had seen, how she hung around Langley. The migraine was better this morning. He said so, and he did look almost his old self again, but Phyllis was full of migraine lore, Mrs. Barker's attacks having apparently genned her up on every aspect.

Langley was off to an auction today, and he must on no account miss a meal. Regular meals were necessary when you had just recovered from a migraine, and if you couldn't get a meal some sugar.

Phyllis produced a bag of barley sugar. She also produced a packed lunch. Sian wouldn't have been surprised to see her bring out a thermos flask full of ice cubes, to be clapped on the temples at the first sign of a recurring twinge.

Barney, drinking coffee, watched with a grin that fanned Sian's exasperation. She knew that Barney, in Langley's position, would have had none of it, but Langley was enjoying the fussing. It probably reminded him of Emily. He took it with a smile, and by the time he and Sian faced each other in the studio she was fixed and firm in her resolution.

She said, 'Before we do the mail, there's something I want to settle. I want Phyllis out.'

'You do?' He was surprised. 'I thought she was managing very well.'

'Too darned well. So well that Natalie came over to warn me last night that Phyllis seems to be making herself indispensable round here.' She put a hand on Langley's arm. 'I don't want her indispensable. Not to you.'

He was pleased. Sian had never shown any jealousy before, and he was flattered. He said, 'There's no fear of that.'

'I don't want to chance it.' She said quietly, 'You asked me to marry you yesterday. Can I answer now?'

He knew her answer. He took her in his arms. 'Sian, oh, my love, I don't really want anyone around here but you, no one else at all.' He kissed her lips and she clung to him.

'I'd like that too. Let's keep them all out.'

She wished they could, and that this moment could last for ever, but time ticked away and the door from the hall opened and shut and Barney came through the studio door. He started to say something, but Langley said, 'Congratulate us, we've just got engaged.'

'Have you now?' He might have looked more surprised after what he'd said last night. Instead he sounded as though he'd been expecting it. 'And good luck to you both,' he said.

Sian smiled, 'You think we'll need it?'

'You might well,' said Barney. He handed Langley a packet. 'From Phyllis. You forgot the barley sugar.'

Sian said, 'You'd better go, darling. Get back as soon as you can.' She kissed Langley. 'I'll look through the stock while you're away.'

For a ring! Langley had just said, 'I must buy you a ring,' and she had pretended to be shocked,

'*Buy* a ring? With all the beautiful things we've got here? I shall pick the biggest in the shop.'

They were all second-hand, of course, and nothing very expensive, but among the Little Gallery's stock of jewellery were some pretty Victorian dress rings. She would select a few, and make a final choice with Langley when he came back from the auction.

After Langley and Barney had gone she stood for a moment, wishing that she didn't have to go in and tell Phyllis. The prospect of hurting was casting a little cloud over her happiness.

Phyllis was through with the washing-up and was sitting at the kitchen table, making out a shopping list. When Sian walked in she said, 'He forgot the barley sugar.'

'He hadn't gone. Barney gave them to him.'

'Good!' Phyllis brightened and began to write 'marmalade' and Sian said,

'I've got something to tell you. Langley and I have just got engaged.'

Phyllis's pencil gave a convulsive shudder. She looked at the squiggle it made as though it was spirit writing. Then she said, 'Why, that's marvellous!'

'Thank you.'

Phyllis had rehearsed this. She knew just what she was going to say. 'I hope you'll both be happy, I'm sure you will.' She was expecting it, she was ready for it, she smiled with stricken eyes and felt she was hiding all.

Sian felt wretched. However she worded this it was going to be hurt on hurt for Phyllis. She said, 'Phyllis, you're not working here because you need the job or the money, are you? You're doing it for Langley, so wouldn't it be better now if you stopped coming?'

'Oh no, please!' Phyllis's lips quivered and her voice was plaintive. 'I won't be in the way, I never thought that Langley was interested in me, but I'm helping, aren't I? Running the house and that. I've always known that you and Langley—' she bit her lip. 'I – I just like being around.'

'There's no future in it.'

166

'I know. I don't expect any. I'm not asking for anything.'

'Do stop being so humble. You ought to be asking for something.'

Phyllis averted her face. 'What's the use? I wouldn't get it if I asked.'

'In this case,' said Sian crisply, 'you would not, so why not try asking for something you might get?'

'Like Gordon? Gordon said I was worse than an old woman. He said I drove him daft, fussing.' She twirled the pencil between her fingers, digging a pin-point hole in her shopping list, and sighed deeply, and Sian could have shaken her. Phyllis was a natural Patient Grizelda and Sian had never taken to Grizelda. But she liked Phyllis, in an exasperated fashion, and her impatience turned on herself.

She said, 'Oh, stay if you want to, but remember it's only a temporary job, not a way of life.'

She went back to the gallery and got on with the mail. Between coming out to serve customers, and answering phone calls, she went over their ring selection, and chose three that she particularly liked. She put them on the typewriter table and pored over them, and when the doorbell rang and it was Barney she turned quickly to get back into the studio, because her instinct was to sweep the rings into a drawer, out of sight.

She didn't. Why should she? The heck with him! Anyhow, he was probably going to the house. But he came into the studio, and she sat with the rings in front of her and said, 'What can I do for you?'

'Not much, I should think.' He looked at the rings. 'Opals are unlucky.'

'Not for me, I'm Libra.'

'Choosing your own?'

'Narrowing the field.' She had one designed like three daisies, with chip rubies surrounded by chip diamonds – that she thought was her favourite. Then the opals, three of them set in a wide bar of gold; and a seed pearl heart.

'And pearls are for tears,' said Barney. 'Have you sacked

Phyllis yet?'

'No, and I'm not going to. She knows the situation, I've told her.'

'No scenes?'

'Nothing for your notebook. You'd have been disappointed, she took it so calmly.'

'Of course she did,' said Barney. 'She knows her place does Phyllis. She's a throwback to Victorian times. In her eyes the master can do no wrong.' He picked up the seed pearl ring, and Sian's hand.

She said, 'What do you think you're—' and he put the ring on her third finger, holding her hand as though it was a piece of display equipment, and surveying the ring critically.

'Pretty,' he said.

'I don't like that one,' she said. She jerked it off and picked up the other two. 'Aren't you working this morning? I should have expected you to be working like mad to catch up with all the hours you wasted while Natalie was here.'

Barney grinned, 'Wasted? You've got to be joking. No, I'm not working, I'm packing.'

'You're going?'

'Yes. I got over to Nelly's room and half-way through the morning I realized I was feeling fine, I've had my convalescence, I'm fit to return to my natural stamping grounds.'

She hoped he was right. His arm was out of the sling, and had been for several days. She said, 'It wouldn't be Natalie? I mean, last time she came you were all for haring back.'

'Last time,' he said, 'I couldn't. This time I can.'

'Yes, well, I presume you know what you're doing. You will wait and say good-bye to Langley, won't you?'

'I shall say good-bye to everybody,' Barney assured her.

'Right,' she said. 'You do that, and I'm sure Phyllis will help with your packing.'

Tommy Poole, of Poole and Sons, funeral directors and cars for hire, arrived outside the Little Gallery at two o'clock, to ferry Barney and his belongings back to London.

Tommy was delighted. He would be staying overnight at Barney's 'pad', returning tomorrow. It was a good fare, and a good night out, and he was grinning like a Cheshire cat.

He hoped Langley wouldn't be too long, because they couldn't leave until Langley came back, but he was a patient man – his profession taught patience – and Sian had rung through and spoken to Langley, and he was coming as quickly as he could.

Langley had said, 'What? Today?' when Sian announced that Barney had decided to leave.

'I don't know what the hurry is – Natalie again, I suppose. Nor why he can't leave it till tomorrow, but that's what he said.'

'That's Barney,' said Langley, resigned if rueful. 'He's stayed longer than I expected him to stay. Try to keep him there till I get back. I'd like to say good-bye. Heaven knows when I'll see him again.'

She'd said, 'I'll keep him here if I have to let the air out of Tommy Poole's tyres.'

Barney might have gone if it hadn't been for Sian – written a note for his brother, thanks for everything and see you some time; and left it like that.

'No, you don't,' Sian said. 'It's bad enough using Langley the way you do, you're not checking out like a hotel and tossing your key on the counter. You're saying good-bye. You're waiting till he gets here.'

Barney waited, but only just. When Langley arrived the stuff was stacked in the car, and Barney and Tommy were in the gallery, watching the road through the large display windows. As Langley drew up they went out to meet him.

He got out of his car, and he and Barney met on the pavement. Langley said, 'This is a sudden decision, isn't it?' Then he amended, 'It would be sudden for me, but not for you, I suppose. You're sure you feel up to it?'

'Quite sure,' said Barney. He put a hand on Langley's shoulder. 'Take care.'

'And you,' said Langley. 'When do we see you again?'

Barney shrugged slightly. 'You know how it is.'

Langley knew. He said, 'You'll come down for the wedding?' Sian stood beside him.

'Maybe,' said Barney. 'When is it going to be?'

Langley turned to Sian. Barney stood waiting, looking at her. She said, 'I – don't know. We haven't fixed a date.'

'Then fix one now,' said Barney. 'In a month's time? In two months?'

Langley still looked at Sian. She said shrilly, 'We can't fix a wedding date like this.'

'Why not?' said Barney. 'You could make it next week and still have time to send out the invitations. Why wait?'

Langley smiled, 'Stop teasing her. But you're right, why wait? We could fix a date.'

Sian said, 'And when we do we'll let you know. It may be old-fashioned, but I'd value a mite of privacy while we're discussing wedding plans. It isn't a bring-and-buy sale.'

'Now there's a gimmick,' said Barney. He said good-bye again, and he got into the car beside Tommy Poole, and waved to the village as he went.

Langley and Sian watched the car vanishing down the long straight high street. Langley said, 'I don't know whether he should have gone back yet.'

Sian thought, he should never have come. He knows too much, he sees too much. . . . 'When it comes to the crunch of truth you don't want to marry Langley . . .' 'I'll marry you,' she had said, but they were only words. To give a date when the words would become irrevocable had been utterly beyond her.

CHAPTER NINE

THE road was very long. Straight through the village and
beyond to where pavements and houses gave way to grass
and trees. They watched until the car took the first distant
bend, and Langley stood there a few moments after Sian
had turned and gone back into the gallery.

As he followed her in she asked, 'How did the auction go?
Did you miss much, having to dash back like this?'

'I got a few things.' He reached for her hand. 'Did you get
a chance to look over the rings?'

'I've had a fairly busy morning.' She drew her hand away.
'I sold the butler's tray and stand, and the pole-screen. And
somebody came in who's collecting pastille burners, and
they're coming back on Friday to tell you what they've got
and what they'd like you to keep an eye open for. And there
were some phone calls.'

She had made notes, as she always did when Langley
wasn't around, and as he read them in the studio she put the
rings back. She felt light-headed with panic. She wanted to
be alone, to creep away somewhere and try to think.
Thoughts and emotions churned together until the result
was physical nausea. She felt ill, and thank heavens it was
nearly closing time.

It had been Phyllis's day for visiting Emily.

When she came back, Langley and Sian were in the display room, and she went straight up to Langley and said her
piece again, 'I hope you'll both be very happy, and I'm sure
you will.'

'Thank you,' said Langley. He smiled affectionately at
Phyllis, and Sian asked,

'How was Emily?'

Phyllis told them what they knew. That Emily was standing now. Not walking by any means, but she had been standing. Phyllis thought Sian looked pale. She said, 'Emily gave

me a special recipe for devilled kidneys, I thought I'd make them for tea. You'll stay for tea today, won't you?'

'No,' said Sian. 'No, thank you.'

Langley had just said, 'We must celebrate tonight, darling. What about the Royal?' and Sian had extemporized wildly.

'I promised I'd spend the evening with Fiona. George is going out, and she gets nervous on her own.'

'Does she?' Langley was surprised to hear that. So was Fiona going to be surprised. And George, who hadn't planned on going any farther than his own living-room. But Sian had to have a quiet evening. She had to have time to think.

She went at half-five, when the aroma of devilled kidneys was beginning to seep into the gallery. She went through George's ground-floor department, where George was selling toothpaste, and he called after her, 'Barney get away all right?'

'At a rate of knots,' she told him. She didn't look back, and she didn't look for Fiona on the first floor. She went quickly up to her own room.

She had made such a mess of things. She had got herself into such an almighty mix-up. How was she going to tell Langley she couldn't marry him, when she'd only told him this morning that she would? 'I've had second thoughts. Third thoughts, actually. First I said "Wait", then I said "Yes", now I'm saying "No, thank you". And you wouldn't want to marry an idiot, would you?'

'Why?' he'd ask. A reasonable question! If only she could provide an answer anywhere as near as reasonable.

She walked around. It didn't help much in the wording of her answer, but she felt too jittery to sit still. When Fiona opened the door she whirled round, and Fiona asked anxiously, 'Are you all right? I thought you looked a bit preoccupied just now.'

'Preoccupied?' Sian moaned. 'I'm going out of my mind!'

Fiona came in. 'Over what?'

'Langley. We got engaged today.' Fiona waited. 'This morning,' said Sian, 'but I can't marry him. I just can't. You'd have thought I'd have known that, wouldn't you, at nine o'clock this morning, considering it's so crystal clear at six o'clock tonight?'

Fiona sat down on the divan, and looked hard at Sian. 'What happened?'

'He asked me to fix a date, and I finally faced what it meant – a whole lifetime of looking after Langley.'

'Would that be so bad?'

'Last night Barney told me I'd got my life so geared to looking after somebody that I couldn't imagine doing anything else with it. I was mad at him, I was sure he was talking rubbish. But he wasn't.' She looked at the curtained archway to Nelly's room as though Barney was standing there, and she begrudged him his triumph.

Fiona said quietly, 'You're not in love with Langley?'

'No.' The word was flat and dull, and spoken with no doubt. 'When I first saw him, and he needed me, I thought it had to be love. It was so right, it was all I was ever going to ask from life, to stay with Langley and make things easy for him.'

'And now?' said Fiona.

'And now,' said Sian, 'I want to run.'

Neither spoke. Then Fiona said, 'Barney won't be back.'

'What's that got to do with it?'

'Nothing,' said Fiona. 'What are you going to tell Langley? He could take this badly. He's very sensitive, this is going to hurt him.'

Fiona was a romantic, with too much compassion for her own peace of mind. She had been pleased at the way things were shaping for Sian and Langley. She had looked forward to having them as friends and neighbours through the years.

But she was too astute not to have seen the change in Sian over these past weeks. The modelling had been the first surprise, revealing a power that Fiona had never suspected.

173

Sian had changed since Barney Hollis came, growing in self-reliance, becoming a vital personality. It was probably inevitable that she should be demanding more from life.

But Barney had gone, and Fiona hoped profoundly that Sian wasn't waiting for him to come back, because he wouldn't. Langley was here, would always be here. She said, 'Poor Langley. He's in love with you, you know,' and Sian said, with a touch of hysteria,

'I hope Phyllis cooked the devilled kidneys exactly like Emily told her, the way Langley likes them. The secret's in how you blend the mustard.' Fiona blinked, and Sian went on, 'You know something else Barney said? That Phyllis is the girl for Langley.' She went across to her model. 'And I am the girl for nobody, except possibly this, and the world may well be my oyster.'

Fiona said tartly, 'Barney seems to have said a lot before he upped and went.'

'Mmm,' Sian agreed. 'One prediction bang on and two to go. That's not bad. He could have the second sight.'

'Or he could be a born troublemaker,' said Fiona with asperity, and Sian nodded again,

'I should think that's more likely.'

'I'll get some tea,' said Fiona.

George was cooking fish fingers, and the kettle was boiling when she got down into the kitchen. She started to tell him, 'Sian's decided she doesn't want to marry Langley after all.' George flipped his fish fingers deftly, with the wrist action of an expert. 'Poor Langley's going to take it badly.'

'Doesn't he know?' asked George.

'No,' said Fiona. 'She's trying to decide how to break it to him.'

George grinned. His streak of compassion was less than Fiona's, and shot with cynicism. 'She'd better break it gently,' said George, 'or she'll be nursing him through a nervous breakdown.'

Fiona took up a cup of tea, and Sian had sleeves rolled up and clay on her hands. Fiona stood beside her, looking at Joss

Ennerman. 'It *is* good,' said Fiona.

'Thank you. I thought I'd ring him and tell him it's finished. It will be by tomorrow.'

Fiona put down the tea. She said, 'I think Barney could be right there too. You could make a name for yourself.'

Sian wrinkled her nose. 'Watch it,' she said, 'or I'll do you next, and they all come out so darned ugly.'

The one of Barney had been uglier than this, but that had been a real caricature, knocked off in a few hours. In this head she had tried to recapture something of the spirit of the man, and she felt she had a little. She wondered if Barney had taken that nonsense head with him. He should be home by now, all his cases unloaded, the typewriter and tape-recorder placed on desk or table or floor, or wherever he kept them.

She wondered if he'd phoned Natalie to tell her he was coming, or waited until he arrived. Natalie *would* be pleased. Natalie would be with him in less than no time, looking like Natalie always looked.

Sian worked on. She missed the sound of the typewriter from the next room, and the faint murmur of a voice. Even when Barney wasn't there, or when they were hardly on speaking terms, there had been a feeling like companionship. Now it was very quiet.

She worked on until the knock on the door, then she called, 'Come in,' and it was Langley, puzzled and accusing.

'I thought you said George was going out.'

She said simply, 'I did, but he wasn't. I wanted to be by myself, it seemed easier to say that than trying to explain why.'

'Easier to lie to me?' said Langley, and she flushed.

'I'm sorry, but yes.'

'Why did you want to be by yourself?'

There was no postponing it, it had to be said now. She said, 'I made a mistake this morning. We wouldn't make a good marriage. We wouldn't make any kind of marriage at all.'

He flinched as though she had struck him, then his mouth

set. 'We would. We will.'

'Listen to me, please. I'm sorry, I've been fooling myself and I suppose I've been fooling you, but I'm wrong for you, Langley. I'm too selfish. I am selfish. I want things for myself.'

'What kind of things?'

'I – oh, I don't know how to put it. I'm just so sure that it wouldn't work.'

'Is it Barney?'

'No.'

'Because if it is you can forget him. He'll have forgotten you already. Next time you see Barney he probably won't remember your name.'

. . . But he would. He made notes, didn't he? Files full of notes and names. . . . She bit hard on her lip. 'It's nothing to do with Barney.' She wiped the clay from her hands, and Langley said,

'You have to take what you can get in this life. You have to compromise, make the best of what you've got.'

'Maybe you do.' She looked at her hands. 'And maybe the best I've got is some sort of talent as a sculptor.'

He crossed to the model. 'You can't give your life to this.'

'I don't want to give my life to anything. I want to live my life.'

She knew he was going to smash it. She watched him lift it and crash it down, and thought he was entitled to that small revenge. She closed her eyes, and felt the breaking like a bruise on her flesh.

Langley didn't turn. He stood, looking down at what he had done, then he said huskily, 'I love you, Sian, I worship the ground you walk on, I'd die for you.'

'Don't, please!'

'I'm sorry,' he gestured at the pieces at his feet, 'I shouldn't have done that. But I do love you, I can't live without you, and you're going to marry me.' He looked at her then, reaching to hold her, imploring, 'Please, Sian, please!'

He was going on his knees to her, and she couldn't bear

that. She begged, 'No, *no* . . .'

'Sian, I worship you.' She stopped her ears and turned her head, and when George opened the door she was blind and dumb for the moment, until Langley loosed her and George said brightly,

'Charades?'

Langley almost ran past him. George stepped aside to let him pass and called, 'Go steady on the stairs!'

She gulped to get her breath back, and put hands on her hair trying to reduce her general dishevelment. 'That's right,' she said, 'charades! Guess the word.'

George grinned his devilish grin. He said, 'I see Langley isn't taking no for an answer.'

'That's the word.'

George's eyebrows went up even higher at the broken model. 'Fiona said your work wasn't his kind of merchandise. If I were you I'd go and daub some tar on that painting he's been doing for the last twelve months.'

She smiled shakily. 'I'm glad you came in. Things were getting out of hand. Did you expect him to smash up the place? If you did it was *very* courageous of you.'

'No,' said George, 'I'm not built for chucking out. I come with words, advice.'

'Then let's hear them.'

He began to stack the clay pieces into a rough heap. He said, 'Don't let Langley blackmail you into marrying him. He'll try it. Emotional blackmail is second nature to him.'

'I thought you liked Langley.'

'I *do*.' George was indignant at any other suggestion. 'I like him very much. It's just that I know him better than most. He's a nice chap, he can't help being helpless. Some women find that very lovable, little Phyllis Barker for one.

'But you wouldn't, would you, in the long run? And Langley would be a weight on your shoulders for the rest of your life.'

He had finished collecting his clay pieces. He got up and looked at Sian, without smiling. 'I know the Hollis boys, because I grew up with them. Round here most folk believe that Langley was the hard-done-by one, but of course he wasn't. Langley stayed put because he lacked the guts to get out. If Barney hadn't the gallery would have been bankrupt years ago. Barney's put a damn sight more money into that place than he'll ever get out of it.

'Langley could well make such a fuss that you marry him. He could convince you, and believe it himself, that he needs you and only you. Well, he doesn't. He needs somebody all right, because he's got no strength of his own. But it would be a waste if it was you when Phyllis Barker would do just as well.'

Sian knew she should be denying this vehemently, but George never overstated things unless he was fooling, and he was serious now. She said, in desperate defence, 'Langley feels things so deeply. When Emily—'

'When Emily fell off her chair,' said George, 'Langley nearly went spare. But check who paid for the private room, and who'll arrange for Emily's convalescence and anything else she needs. In Langley's case words speak louder than actions. When Mr. Hollis was dying it was Barney he called for.'

'And Barney didn't get there until he was dead.'

'No.' He looked as if he wondered how she knew. 'Because there was a fog that night, you couldn't see your hand in front of you. It took him twelve hours to get through from London.'

'Langley must have forgotten. He told me Barney just didn't come.'

'*Forgotten?*' said George incredulously. He thought about it. 'I don't know, though, it was a bad night for Langley, waiting for his father to die; he *might* have forgotten a fog outside. On the other hand, whether he knows it or not, he is jealous of Barney. If I was a psychiatrist I'd be inclined to think that subconsciously he'd prefer the memory of Barney deliberately arriving late.'

She said, in a dazed voice, 'You make Langley sound as if he needs a psychiatrist.'

'I shouldn't think so,' said George. 'At least if he does so do a good many other folk. He'll make a good husband for the right girl. He'll be devoted, and she'll always be needed. Looking after Langley's going to be somebody's full-time occupation.' He grinned again. 'It's just that I can't see you settling for it for ever. I may be wrong. I simply give you the facts for what they're worth, so that you know what you'd be letting yourself in for.'

She said, 'Thank you.'

'You're welcome,' said George. In the doorway he said, 'Fiona doesn't agree. She thinks that Langley is the lad to lean on.'

'And you think she's wrong?'

'I know,' said George, 'that if she married Langley, Fiona would clobber him over the head with a coal scuttle within the first month.'

When George had gone Sian took the wastepaper basket over and dropped in Joss Ennerman's head from the pile, piece by piece. She had made a very creditable shot at his mouth. She was sorry to see that go. She thought, I'll start again tomorrow. I'll do it all over again.

She would ring Ennerman, explain that there had been an accident, but she was working, and she would have something for him soon.

She thought a great deal about what George had just said. The more she considered it the more probable it seemed.

Dear Langley, with his charm and his sympathy and his need. He needed caring for, cherishing, and for some women that would be enough. But Sian knew her own independent spirit, and she realized that between them the day would come when Langley would be impossibly demanding of help, when he would cling to her like a gentle vampire draining her life away.

So whatever happened tomorrow she must stay firm. Whether he pleaded or argued she mustn't weaken.

Almost certainly she would have to leave here. She was sorry about that. She would like to have stayed and worked in the gallery, doing her modelling in this room next to

Nelly's room, but that depended on Langley. If he made it impossible she would get out at once.

Anyhow, she thought that a short holiday was called for, so she rang Mrs. Griggs and was invited on the spot. She got out a suitcase and put in a few things, then left it open against the wall to be completed when her plans were more definite.

She looked in on Fiona and George after the phone call, to tell them. George was puffing away at his pipe, and Fiona had the tense expression of a girl who has been longing for ages to rush in where angels kept out. George had said firmly, 'Leave her alone,' and Fiona was biding her time till George went down to the ground floor to get some more tobacco, which he would have to do before long if he intended to go on smoking, then she was rushing upstairs to check on Sian.

When Sian looked in Fiona was relieved to see her smiling. The smile was strained round the eyes, but it was a good sign, and Fiona said heartily, 'Come and have a nice stiff drink.'

'I think I'd better keep a clear head,' said Sian, 'I may be going to need one tomorrow. I've just used your phone.' She told them why, and they agreed that getting away for a while would be the smart coward's way out. She said sadly, 'I'll have to leave the gallery, because after this it would be embarrassing all round if I went on working there.'

George chuckled and Fiona glared at him. 'You'll get yourself another job easy as pie,' said George. 'And near enough to go on living here. I tell you one thing, I'm not getting that rocking horse down again.'

They cheered her up wonderfully. They helped her plan her future, and George made her phone Joss Ennerman.

Ennerman said he had been waiting to hear from her, and what did she mean, 'an accident'? She said, 'It got knocked off.' He growled an obscenity, and she said, 'But I think I've got my priorities right now. I promise I'm going to work very hard.'

'See you do,' he said. 'Is Barney there?'

'No, he went back to London.'

From the phone, on the first floor, she looked up to the rooms under the eaves, her room and Nelly's room. It was hard to believe that Barney had gone. She could almost see him moving among the shadows at the top of the stairs.

Long ago he had phoned Natalie on this phone and Sian had heard him say, 'You'll never know how much I miss you.' She said good-bye to Joss Ennerman now, and replaced the phone, and stood still and quiet before she went back to George and Fiona.

She was missing Barney, with a queer little ache. He was the kind of person who was bound to leave an emptiness when he wasn't there any more. It would go away before long. Of course it would. It must, because everybody knew that Barney wasn't coming back for months. After his enforced stay, maybe not for years. He had had enough of this backwater, the times he had said that.

She hurried to Fiona and George, to tell them what Joss Ennerman had said.

She woke just after six o'clock next morning, and it was going to be a grim day. She wished she could have closed her eyes again and declined any part of it, but Langley had to be faced and the day had to be faced, and she sat up in bed and sighed.

She would have given a great deal to have had Barney around today, to take some of the grimness out of it. She would have liked to talk to Barney.

She went down into the empty shop and dialled his number, surprised to find that she knew it by heart. She had never phoned it before, but of course it was in the phone book at the gallery, and there must have been some reason why this particular combination of figures had fixed itself in her mind. Maybe they tied in with a date, or did they run consecutively? There had to be an explanation. Anyhow, she did remember them.

Ten past six was a bit early for chatting. She realized that as she listened to the bell ringing, then she shrugged because she'd done it now. It was too late to get considerate.

Natalie answered, yawning the number as though she had been asleep and had stretched out a groping hand to lift the receiver, and Sian put her own phone down again.

She went back to her room. She finished packing her case. At the latest she'd be leaving tomorrow. Today she would have to see Langley again. She should really try to see Emily. She would be away for two, three weeks, and she'd do some modelling while she was away; and then she'd have to see about another bread-and-butter job while she went on with her modelling.

Like George said it should be easy enough for her to get something in town and go on living here. She liked living here. Fiona and George would be very, very hard to re-place.

She cooked breakfast so that when Fiona and George came down it was ready, and she'd cleared out the ashes of the stove, and Fiona said, 'You *have* been busy. What time were you up and about?'

'Oh, an hour or so ago. Can I have breakfast with you?'

She had always had breakfast over at the gallery, but obviously not this morning. 'Draw up,' said Fiona expansively. 'This is luxury. We can linger over breakfast like the leisured classes.'

Sian found that she couldn't eat. The first mouthful almost choked her, so that she coughed and spluttered and George had to thump her back. She apologized, 'Sorry, I suppose it's what's ahead of me. I'm dreading today.'

'You'll get through it,' said George.

'Yes, of course.' She felt very old and tired, as though her blood ran sluggishly and would never sing again.

'It's not the end of the world,' said George cheerfully.

'Oh, I do hope not,' said Sian. But if it had been she could hardly have felt a blacker depression. The end of everything just about summed up the way she felt right now.

She said, 'I want to go today. I really do need to get away for a while, but do you think I should wait until Langley can find someone else for the gallery?'

'Make that offer,' said George, 'and you'll be stuck with

it. Let Phyllis serve in the shop.'

'Phyllis can't type.'

'Langley can. Let Langley type his own letters,' said George with feeling. 'I have to.'

Sian had no idea what kind of reception she was going to get over at the gallery. She let herself in as usual. She was a little later today, within minutes of opening time, but the mail was still on the mat, and she picked it up and took it with her.

In the kitchen Phyllis and Langley sat at table. Langley was finishing his breakfast, and Phyllis was pouring him another cup of coffee, and they both smiled at Sian.

Langley was playing it cool. When he said, 'Good morning, darling,' and got up to kiss her, the prospect of last night's scene all over again was too much.

She couldn't face it. She sat down and said, 'I'm going away today. I shall be away for a few weeks, and do please get someone else to take over my job in the gallery.'

Phyllis dropped the coffee pot, miraculously without scalding herself. Langley said, 'If you need a holiday of course you must have one, but no one else takes your job here. That will be waiting for you.'

'I won't be coming back to it. I meant what I said last night.'

It would have been more civilized not to say this in front of anyone but Langley, but Phyllis was an avidly interested party, and Sian was beyond ethics.

Langley said, 'I'll take the mail into the studio, I'll see you in there.'

'No!' She wasn't leaving any half-finished miniatures. She was leaving nothing that someone else couldn't handle; and she was prolonging this conversation not a minute more than she had to. She said, 'I want to go now, Langley.'

He could hardly have looked with greater reproach if he had caught her poisoning his coffee.

...'Emotional blackmail is second nature to Langley,' George had told her ...

'Go if you must,' said Langley, 'but if you don't come

back to me I shall kill myself.'

Phyllis shrieked. Sian said wearily, 'Don't be such a fool.'

'I mean it. I can't live without you.' He went, closing the door behind him, and Phyllis wailed,

'How could you? Oh, how could you do this to Langley?'

'I don't know,' said Sian. 'It's surprising me too.'

'You're wicked! Oh, you're a wicked woman! Can't you see you're breaking his heart?'

Sian got up off her chair. She said, 'He's all yours.'

'Oh!' said Phyllis. She followed Sian into the gallery, and watched her put down her key on one of the tables, and go out into the street. Phyllis shook her head. This was terrible. They must have had a quarrel last night, and Sian wasn't forgiving. But how she could do a thing like this to Langley? Phyllis shook her head again, and picked up the key, and by the time she tapped on the studio door she had stopped smiling.

Sian had twenty minutes before she could catch a bus that would take her to the hospital to say good-bye to Emily, so she looked into the store to tell George and Fiona where she was going, and buy a box of chocolates.

There were no customers on the ground floor, and as George reached down the chocolates Sian said, 'Langley says he's going to kill himself. He wouldn't carry pique that far would he? I know he won't do it, but I mean he wouldn't – well, pretend to do it?'

George put the chocolates on the counter. 'Possibly,' he said. 'Pretend, I mean. I'll keep an eye on him.' He grinned, 'I'll tell him he's well rid of you.'

'And he is,' said Sian. 'Like Fiona, I'd have ended by clouting him with a coal scuttle.'

Emily was sorry, but less surprised than she might have been, and less distressed. Phyllis Barker was second choice on Emily's list, but her opinion of Phyllis had risen lately. If Sian was adamant she was glad there was Phyllis.

Her room was still full of Natalie's roses; the whole nursing home seemed full of them, they were lasting well.

Emily said, 'You will come back, though, won't you? After you've had a holiday,' and Sian bent to kiss her.

'You haven't seen the last of me.'

Emily said gently, 'You look as if you could do with a holiday. You look about all in.'

The bus got Sian back before lunch time, and she wasn't hanging around. She would have a quick snack, then phone for a taxi, and go. She did need a holiday. She was all in.

As she went through George's department he smiled at her with immense good humour, and she managed to smile back. Fiona didn't smile. She was serving, and she watched Sian climb the stairs as apprehensively as though there was a banana skin on one of them.

Sian caught herself listening. She wasn't going to hear a typewriter. She knew that, it was habit; and she didn't. Her eyes were smarting. The strain of last night and this morning was taking toll. She would weep, if she let herself.

She blinked, and her vision blurred as she opened the door. Again, harder, shock hitting her so that she swayed; and her eyes cleared and it was Barney sitting on the divan. And before he spoke or moved she knew in a flash of blinding intensity that she loved him.

She said – or someone using her voice said – 'What are you doing here?'

'I left something behind.'

He got up, and she walked quite well considering, and whoever was using her voice said, 'You should have phoned. We'd have sent it on.'

'It might have been awkward to pack. It was you.'

He wasn't smiling, although that had to be a joke. She sat in the first chair she reached, and Barney stood and watched her. He said, 'Did you know I'd be back?'

'How could I know?'

He smiled then, but his eyes were dark. 'A good question. So I'll tell you why – I can't go without you. Anywhere. I've got to have you right here with me, or in the next room, or across the road. No further away.'

He still smiled. 'If you're not around I'm lost. I've never

been so lonely in my life as I was last night.'

'You had Natalie. She was with you.' She had been frozen since she heard Natalie, saying Barney's number in that sleepy voice. She had walked and talked, and carried ice in her veins, numbing a pain that couldn't be borne. Now she was turning back into flesh and blood, and jealousy clawed and ripped. She said, 'I phoned you. Natalie answered.'

'When did you phone me?'

'Six o'clock this morning. She was there. She answered.'

'No one told me you phoned.'

'I hung up when she answered.'

He said, 'It wasn't Natalie. She went home long before that. It could have been anybody. There was a welcome-back party, and those who couldn't have faced a breathalyser dossed down. I took Natalie home, and then walked around the streets for the rest of the night.'

A girl's voice. It didn't have to be Natalie. She had just taken it for granted it was Natalie.

Barney said, 'Why did you phone me?'

'I wanted to talk to you. I missed you.'

'How much?'

She admitted at last, to herself and to him, 'I stopped living. That much.'

'Limbo!' he said. 'No colour, no light, no reason. I suppose a man could exist without them, but he couldn't live. And when you're not around neither are they.'

She went into his arms and he kissed her, and she had wings so that she could skim the stars and the weight of the world fell away.

They smiled at each other. Two who had stars for stepping stones, sharing the wonder. She traced the scar on his face with a finger tip. 'I don't think you're ever going to lose that completely. You did make a mess of yourself, didn't you?'

'As it happens,' he said, 'I always looked more or less like this. From now on of course I shall blame it on the smash-up, but I'll tell you because I love you.'

'I knew it,' she said. 'I've seen pictures of you. You were an ugly little boy.'

'And you're beautiful,' he said. 'Oh, God, you are beautiful!'

'Not as beautiful as Natalie.' She would never be jealous of Natalie again, nor of any woman breathing, but Natalie Wender was fashioned like the roses. The one-in-a-million miracle in the human race.

Barney nodded. 'She's beautiful,' he said. 'And she can act. She could end up pretty near the top. And last night I couldn't shove her through her front door fast enough.'

'But you were in love with her? When you asked her to come down, when you wanted to go back with her.'

He said wryly, 'I was getting away from you. I'd just begun to suspect that I was heading for something out of my ken. I wasn't over-easy about it.

'What I didn't realize was that if I'd gone, even then, I'd have crawled back. Within a week of meeting you I couldn't have lasted long without you.'

Langley had said, 'I can't live without you,' but not like this, the words echoing deep inside her as though they were the core of her being. She said huskily, 'I – believe you.'

'You'd better believe it, lady.' He stroked her hair and his fingers trembled. 'You're going to be living with it for the rest of your life. You'll marry me?'

It was a question where there was no need for questions. She nodded.

'When?'

'Any day.'

She was even packed. He looked at the case as she did. 'Where were you going?' he said.

'I don't think I was going. I think I was coming to you.'

If not this week, next week. She couldn't have lasted long without him. She said, 'Did George and Fiona know you were waiting up here for me?'

'Yes.'

She began to smile. 'George approved, but Fiona was a bit fearful. She likes you, but she doesn't altogether trust you with an impressionable girl like me.' Laughter bubbled in her. 'I doubt if she'll leave it much longer before she comes up and offers us some lunch.'

Barney began to laugh too. 'Right,' he said. 'Let's go down and tell her I've been propositioning you, and the wedding's on Friday, and if she's got the stuff in stock the bride wants a trousseau out of the boutique.'

Have You Missed Any of These
Harlequin Romances?

Have You Missed Any of These
Harlequin Romances?

All books listed 75c

Harlequin Romances are available at your local bookseller,
or through the Harlequin Reader Service, M.P.O. Box 707,
Niagara Falls, N.Y. 14302; Canadian address: 649 Ontario St.,
Stratford, Ontario N5A 6W4.

Have you missed any of these . . .

Harlequin Presents..

- ☐ 107 PAGAN HEART, Rebecca Caine
- ☐ 108 PRIDE AND POWER, Anne Hampson
- ☐ 109 TEMPORARY WIFE, Roberta Leigh
- ☐ 110 WITCHSTONE, Anne Mather
- ☐ 111 SUCH IS LOVE, Mary Burchell
- ☐ 112 THE WATERFALLS OF THE MOON, Anne Mather
- ☐ 113 MAN OF GRANITE, Lilian Peake
- ☐ 114 PALACE OF THE POMEGRANATE Violet Winspear
- ☐ 115 THE FAIR ISLAND, Anne Hampson
- ☐ 116 DARK INTRUDER, Nerina Hilliard
- ☐ 117 PRINCE FOR SALE, Rachel Lindsay
- ☐ 118 THE BARTERED BRIDE, Margaret Rome

All books listed are available at **95c each** at your local bookseller or through the Harlequin Reader Service.

Have you missed any of these . . .

Harlequin Presents..

All books listed 95c

Harlequin Presents novels are available at your local bookseller, or through the Harlequin Reader Service, M.P.O. Box 707, Niagara Falls, N.Y. 14302; Canadian address: 649 Ontario St., Stratford, Ontario   N5A 6W4.